Vampire Owner's Manual

by

Tim Forder

Published by
Melange Books, LLC
White Bear Lake, MN 55110
www.melange-books.com

Vampire Owner's Manual ~ Copyright © 2013 by Tim Forder

ISBN: 978-1-61235-680-8 print

Cover Art by Caroline Andrus

Vampire Owner's Manual
Tim Forder

As a skirt-chasing gambler from the old west, I met a beautiful older woman who made wild passionate love with me and then in the heat of passion turned me into a Vampire!

I wrote this Vampire Owner's Manual for those who have just became one of the honored, or is thinking of becoming one of the honored or just want to know more about Vampires.

The Vampire Owner's Manual contains vast knowledge of the Vampire Lore; from proper feeding to staying alive or undead; from Vampire history to Vampire myths and a lot more!

The Vampire Owner's Manual is peppered heavily with personal experience as well as experiences gathered interviewing other Vampires (not an easy task).

When you were born your parents most likely wished you came with an owner's manual. Suddenly you have awakened with a pain in your neck and a ravenous appetite no food will quench; you are having vague memories of "Vampires" from an old movie and you wish you could have a Vampire owner's manual: Well, here it is!

"I bid you ... Welcome"
Dracula, Bela Lugosi, 1931

"...for the blood is the life ..."
Holy Bible: Deut. 12:23
Dracula, Bela Lugosi, 1931

* * * * *

ACKNOWLEDGMENTS

I would like to thank my creative daughter, Ellie, for shooting and improving the author photo!
I would like to thank my whole family for their support in this endeavor.
Mom, thanks for proofreading the college thesis version. Sorry for the many nights without sleep that followed.
I would like to thank Sammi Bold for her contributing art work.

TABLE OF CONTENTS

INTRODUCTION

So you think you are a VAMPIRE. Really? Tell me, how was that pizza and beer you had for lunch? Was it really great; nice, hot and spicy sweet pizza followed by the superbly splendid, always pleasing cold beer—CLOSE THIS BOOK! YOU'RE NOT A VAMPIRE!

Did that great pizza taste like cardboard and leave you thirsty for a big cold beer? Did you then down that beer, finding yourself still thirsty? Did you follow that up by downing the whole six-pack? Still thirsty, you followed the first six-pack with another six-pack? The result being that you find yourself still thirsty, sober and wanting more? Then, Vampire, you had better jump to CHAPTER 1: FEEDING.

(If the pizza tasted like cardboard and the beer quenched your thirst, I would suggest you close this book and stop buying Domino's Pizza!)

Have you suddenly discovered your eyes are so sensitive to light that you have to wear shades…indoors? Did you have to move the pizza away from you because you were overwhelmed by the smell? I recommend you read CHAPTER 2: LIVING OR UNDEAD—especially before you try going outside in the daylight!

If you do find yourself tormentingly thirsty and your eyesight, hearing and sense of smell eerily sensitive—Congratulations! You're a VAMPIRE!

HOLD THE PHONE! You may not be a Vampire. You may have developed a rare blood disorder where your blood can't replenish itself (like a Vampire), or you have developed an allergy to sunlight or fluorescent light. See CHAPTER 3: ILLNESSES THAT MIMIC VAMPIRISM

Now that we have the more important matters out of the way, it is time to learn about your new life or undead life: Enjoy the following chapters and learn all about your new lifestyle as a Vampire.

If you have gone through this introduction and learned that you are not a Vampire but have discovered an interest to learn more about them, feel free to read on.

Feel free not to read if you are a Vampire Hunter and looking to learn more about your prey!

So why would a Vampire write a book about Vampires? Basically so you, a young Vampire, will not have to learn how to keep going the hard way like I had to; so you can learn how to have a normal, happy existence as a Vampire.

As Vampires go, I am very young, only about a hundred or so. Can't say for sure 'cause as a walking blood bag (human), a gambler and skirt chaser (okay, skirt-chasing gambler), I took little time to notice things like what year it was. I only became interested in things like the year and what was going on historically during the Civil War years.

I was born the sixth child of eight to a Missouri dirt farmer. We seldom had much to eat or wear. Mother did make a point of giving us some book learning from books she was given as payment for patching clothes for other farm families. I grew up with no interest in becoming a dirt farmer like my father. Hunting for food to help feed the family revealed a natural way with guns, but I really didn't see myself shooting for a living either.

Finally, I heard a rancher was looking for cowhands to move his herd to market, so I jumped at the chance for a new life. Even though clothes, boots and horse tack all had to come out of my pay before even getting started, Mr. McClintock took me on.

This was going to be a long drive. Seems the California gold rush had created a beef market neither the locals nor the Mexican government alone could handle. Word was if you could get the beef to market in California, it would pay well. One hand asked, "How long will all this take?" The answer, "As long as it takes. Just remember, when you sign on, you sign on 'til the end of the drive." It didn't take long for me to learn that herding cows was a tough job, especially on the sit-upon if you're not horse-wise.

Except for trigger-happy Jack and later some border trouble which required some gunplay, the trip was fairly uneventful. Jack, a tenderfoot like me, was on night duty when he reportedly saw a mountain lion or a wolf stalking the cattle. Believing it his job to protect the herd, he drew his saddle gun and fired off a shot at the beast. The cattle spooked and stampeded. It took us days to get the cattle rounded up again, and Jack was given the boot...literally!

Weeks later, at some unknown border (unknown to us cowhands), we were stopped by a committee that wanted to charge us to pass through their border. McClintock ordered a stampede. "We'll re-gather the herd on the other side." During the racing mayhem of a stampeding herd, I made a strong point to stay in the saddle. Lose your horse in that mayhem and lose your life to hundreds of angry hooves!

At some point, I caught sight of an hombre taking a deadly bead on me over his rifle; I quickly drew my sidearm and let loose two shots. The first must have been let go too soon, as it went wild; the second shot hit the hombre right in the chest. I saw the bloody explosion as the .45 penetrated his chest, then I saw him tossed backward off his horse. Not seeing anyone else taking aim on me, I continued the fight, making sure to stay (alive) on my horse! Couldn't help but hope that hombre was already dead before he was tossed off his horse, for his sake.

Later that night over the dinner fire, I thanked the young hand who befriended me and took the time to teach me how to use my newly acquired side-iron before the run got started; I believe he told me his name was William Bonney (years later someone told me he was better known as "Billy the Kid"). That day I learned just how good I was with a side-iron, given to me at the start of the run by Mr. McClintock himself. I also learned I had no qualms about killing some hombre who was shooting at me!

The job was the toughest job I ever had, and by sheer grit, I made it to the end of the trail to find myself in a cow town with a lot of money burning a hole in my pocket. While getting a drink at one of the two saloons and gambling houses, I got to view my first game of poker. After one of the ex-cowhands I had been traveling with was relieved of his funds and left the game, a fancy-Dan duded up in the fanciest duds I had ever seen invited me to join the game!

After watching the other cowhand lose his grubstake, I might not have taken fancy-Dan up on his invite, but he sounded like he was daring me, and I couldn't let this fancy-Dan up me; so I joined the game. It was addicting; first winning money, then losing money and then having to continue to play to get my money back!

Come morning, I was $400 richer and a confirmed gambling man. Come the next night I was the fancy-Dan in my new duds controlling the poker table and (more importantly) continuing to win.

As many young men are want to do, I spent the evenings bedding the fallen doves of both saloons and gambling houses.

One day, while coming out of the hotel where I had my current room, I walked right into a woman strolling beside the building. I almost knocked the pretty lady down. However, I quickly recovered and grabbed the lady to keep her from an embarrassing scene with her butt on the boardwalk. She wasn't bad looking, so after introducing myself, I invited her to have lunch with me. After looking me over, she invited me to have lunch with her in her home instead. After a great lunch, we had dessert in the bedroom, with her husband's picture looking on.

After a while, I tired of the town and the same old women, both fallen doves and fallen wives. I moved on to the next town, and the next gambling table, and the next fallen women, et cetera.

One day, when the cards were cold and Lady Luck wasn't with me, I left the tables early and literally ran into the most beautiful woman I had ever seen. She was a shapely, blue-eyed blonde in a blue and white rig that showed off her eyes delightfully, not to mention her figure. We talked, and after an enchanting conversation, I mentioned that I had been looking to get some lunch and asked if she could recommend a good place to eat. I also asked if she might have lunch with me. She looked to be considering it and said she'd only agree if we had lunch at her place. "There is no place that has better cooking in this town than my place." How could I possibly pass that up? Maybe "Lady" Luck had returned. It was later that I discovered that "Lady Luck" was fickle!

We were enjoying a very passionate dessert on her wedding bed of five years when the bedroom door smashed open and her husband rushed in with his peacemaker blazing away. Fortunately, for me, he fired high and I was able to roll to reach my fancy silver and pearl handled piece. I fired true, and hit him twice in the chest and once in the face. He was surely dead before he plunged backward out the doorway and hit the floor as a bloody rag pile.

Even before my lovely dessert informed me that her dead husband was the local marshal's brother, I knew I was going to have to vamoose out of the territory and fast. As I rose, I saw the bloodstained deputy star on his ruined chest.

There was most likely paper on me "Dead or Alive: For murder" in Texas before I even made it across the US/Mexican border. Once in Mexico, I was beyond the long arm of the US law.

Within Mexico proper, I eventually came across this small Mexican town with one saloon. Didn't look like the type of saloon I'd find a game in, but a saloon, any saloon, served up drinks. On entering, I ordered a bottle to drain my mouth of trail dust and had no trouble finding a table in the empty place. I was studying the painting over the bar. While trying to figure out what was not quite right with the subject's teeth, the painting's subject, a raven-haired beauty, delivered my bottle with two glasses.

Figure 1 Vampire Beauty. Property of the author

"Would the fancy dressed man like some company?" the beauty asked in accented English.

How could I say no? After we finished the bottle over pleasant conversation, she said, "Would the Mister like sharing a very special bottle with me? It's up in my room."

How could I pass that up?

After we emptied her personal bottle, we made good use of her soft sheets. Just as I was about to come with this ravenous beauty straddling me as if I was her favorite horse, she leaned down and gave me the softest kiss. Just as I was losing it to sexual bliss, I felt two pinpricks enter my neck and suddenly I exploded in total sexual bliss.

Later, after I awoke, I learned that my "lady" love was a Vampire and, no, I would not die from her feeding on me and, no, I would not become a Vampire from our trysting. Maybe I should have shot out of there like a bullet out of a peacemaker, but after what I had experienced, I was ready for more.

We spent days, and nights, in that hot little room, making it hotter—I didn't care! Then one night it happened. While feeding on me, she got carried away and continued taking my blood. After a while, I could feel my heart straining. I could literally feel my life draining into my Vampire lover!

I WAS DYING AND I DIDN'T CARE!

When she finished, she took one look at me and realized she had taken too much of my blood; because of her, I was dying!

She cut open one of her voluptuous naked breasts and said softly, "My love, I have overfed and you are dying. Please take of my blood and live." With that, she brought my mouth up to her soft, abundant breast and gave me a new life!

Afterwards, she explained that with the drinking of her blood, I became a Vampire. She began my rudimentary training in a new lifestyle. A day later, she was gone. The odd thing was I no longer had any interest in the woman with whom I had been so madly in love.

You see, Vampires are basically lone wolves. Even Vampires who go to bars and clubs don't go to associate with other Vampires; we basically only go to feed. It's one of those oddities of Vampire living. Once you turn your lover in to a Vampire, you can't stand to be around them!

Eventually I got lonely for the great USA and roamed back north by way of New Mexico, where there was no paper on me so I had no problems with the law, but made a point of staying out of Texas. To this day, a hundred some years later, I still stay out of Texas, despite the fact that if there's still paper out on me it must be old, yellowed parchment hardly readable.

I discovered this easy meal plan: during the Civil War, after a typical battle between two armies, I could find more meals than I could consume. I really got clever and started posing as a "bone cutter," and if someone spotted me eating over a dying soldier, it would seem as if I were working over a dying soldier. The bad news is that wars don't last forever; the good news is that you never have to wait long for the next war!

I continued my after battle smorgasbord meal plan all through WWI, WWII, The Korean War and the Vietnam War. I have to admit, I enjoyed feeding on the dying during the Civil War (not to mention WWI, WWII, the Korean War, and the Vietnam War.) I felt righteous about feeding on the enemy, but I was a very young, naive, improperly trained Vampire at the time! Reading this Vampire Owner's Manual and heeding its words should prevent such improper behavior while feeding!

Vampires are lone wolves by nature. When it comes to living with blood bags, this is understandable because we don't age and they do. How do you hide the fact from your beloved blood bag that you're not aging? It's just as easy not to get close to your meals! I have gotten around this by living the life of a roaming gambler, never staying in one place too long. Always too busy sampling the spoiled doves to get lonely.

When I'm not researching material for this "Vampire Owner's Manual," it's back to gambling. If the cards are good to me I'll dine at Vampire Clubs, if the cards are not good to me—there's always the Vampire bars. With our heightened sense of smell, neither is hard to find no matter what town or city you have just blown into.

Vampires just see other Vampires as competition for food and easily come to loathe other Vampires by nature. So if you solve the problem of the aging loved one by turning them, within days you will find yourself loathing them instead of loving them. My Beloved Vampire after turning me only had time to give me some basics on my new lifestyle before she mysteriously disappeared, leaving me unprepared.

Years later, I found the boot on the other foot. I fell in love with my meal and after turning her suddenly found myself loathing her and totally not interested in teaching her about her new lifestyle! This event and what happened to me after I was turned gave me the idea to write this *Vampire Owner's Manual.*

CHAPTER ONE
FEEDING

So you suddenly find yourself incredibly hungry or thirsty, but raiding the refrigerator is a total waste of time. The uncooked meat looks incredibly good, but you find you can't eat it either. You enjoyed the bloody juice, but you still need more ... that's because you're a Vampire and your body can no longer replenish itself. Now, you need new blood from an outside source.

If you are reading this and suddenly you're cringing at the thought of attacking people, or "walking blood bags" as some Vampires call human beings, for their blood, STOP CRINGING AND READ ON.

Many graveyard shift meat grocers know about Vampires' needs, and will be glad to sell you a container or two of beef or pig blood that they saved for their special nocturnal customers. If you are still a Living Vampire, you could try this during the day, but the meat grocer may not know enough about Vampires and, at best, will laugh at you; at worst, they will call for help to have you thrown out.

Also, grocery stores are much busier during the day. Are you really going to be able to focus on beef or pig's blood among a bunch of walking blood bags? Remember. At all times, keep your Vampire identity a secret! You don't want to catch the attention of a Vampire Hunter. The exceptions to keeping your identity a secret would be at Vampire bars and clubs.

Some Vampire bars and clubs specialize in providing fresh, warm blood and have a supply of walking blood bags that get off on being your provider. In time, you will be able to find these places by following your heightened Vampire senses. I strongly recommend you resist such places until you have developed enough Vampire maturity to feed without killing. I have seen Vampires who fell into the Vampire stereotype of feeding to the point of killing, then living—or unliving—in constant remorse, until it grows so heavy a burden that the Vampire commits suicide. I know of one such case where a Living Vampire with feed-killing remorse committed suicide and found she had to kill herself twice. She did the traditional cutting of the wrists in the bathtub and bled to death. Then she discovered she was now an Undead Vampire who was suffering from lack of blood. She unlived the torment of hundreds of years in one night, waiting for the sun to come up. (If you are unclear on the living, unliving (undead) read CHAPTER 2: LIVING OR UNDEAD.)

Vampire Bars

Vampire Bars look like normal bars on the outside, with a bartender to serve drinks to the living. The place is usually very dark except near the bar itself. This area of light is for the visual comfort of walking blood bags; the darkened area away from the bar is for the comfort of the Vampire patrons (and their sensitive night sight). The darkened area also provides comfort to the squeamish walking blood bags who like to be fed on, but do not want to see it happening to them or to those around them.

Some Vampire bars have a few rooms for those who feel the need for additional privacy. After all, most walking blood bags are there because they get a sexual high from being fed on, but may have problems with public sex. Some Vampires also have problems with public feeding for the same reason. Vampire bars do not require membership fees, so your blood bag meal tends to be potluck walk-ins. Your higher-class meals are found in Vampire clubs (see below).

One big advantage of a Vampire bar over a Vampire club: you get a free meal. The walking blood bags are there for the thrill of being fed on, so most are more than willing to participate. For this reason, I have attended various Vampire bars for *a bite* when Lady Luck has turned her back on me at the gambling tables and left me short of funds.

A Note on Fresh Feeding

IT'S GREEAAT! I mean… Beef and pig blood are good and get the job done, but blood from any container (other than a Walking Blood Bag) is a little flat. Fresh feeding can make dining a real treat. Nothing like properly seasoned blood, generously laced with adrenaline or endorphins from a walking blood bag garnished with fear or sexual delight.

Unfortunately, there are Vampires (usually undead) who "go to the dark side" for the easy carefree joy of feeding on fearful, dying blood bags. Despite what you see in the movies, this IS NOT appropriate Vampire behavior. It is important that you know Vampires DO NOT try to attract undue, unfavorable attention that could cause a rebirth of Vampire hunting that occurred with the release of Bram Stoker's <u>Dracula</u> or the hunting fervor of the 16th century that almost wiped out all Vampires who were blamed for causing the Black Plague!

Alternate Ways to Acquire a Meal

If you must feed on the dying to get your feeding thrills, become a soldier. After a good battle, it's smorgasbord time! Be careful not to be seen feeding on poor, unlucky injured soldiers.

The Civil War drew my interest when I realized that as a soldier, I had great access to sources of blood from the dying! Under normal circumstances, feeding from a walking blood bag even to the point of death can be fulfilling except for two things: 1) the guilt of killing and 2) the strong possibility of attracting attention from Vampire Hunters.

But on the battlefield, feeding off the dying negates the guilt of killing for food because your food is already dying and death on a battlefield is too common to attract the attention of a Vampire Hunter.

I did have one frightening turn I will never forget. I was shot up bad and in my innocence, I feared bleeding to death. NOTE: Vampires can't bleed to death, but they can bleed to the point of weakness that can cause slow recovery, weakness and the pain of extreme thirst.

Fearing immediate death by loss of blood, I grabbed up a soldier dying of chest wounds and began feeding off his neck. I did not notice that my open wounds were leaking into his open wounds, and a sharing of blood was happening. I did not realize a turning was underway until I tasted the change in his blood. I quickly grabbed an officer's sword lying nearby and decapitated the nearly new Vampire; throwing his head into a running river.

Did I fight for the Blue or the Gray? Yes. Occasionally I would get shot up so bad I would fake death, steal the identity of someone else and continue on. More times than I can recall, the new identity (and the uniform) was from the opposing army. I didn't care what uniform I was wearing; I was fighting for my after-battle feedings, not patriotic idealism!

For a long time I posed as a bone cutter. Wartime surgeons were known as bone cutters because amputation was the most common surgery of the Civil War. As a bone cutter, people who saw me leaning over a dying soldier feeding would assume I was busy examining a patient. After one battle, I was caught feeding. The interloper was wearing the uniform of the other side. I was still trying to decide if I should kill him outright or feed on him when he smiled showing his extracting fangs! He was just another Vampire looking for an after battle meal or two, like me. I grinned back, showing off my fangs and we both got a big laugh over the situation. We shook hands, and went our way to continue our dining. After all, there was enough on the field of battle for an army of Vampires to dine. When the war ended, I was in a blue uniform, not that it mattered. The war wasn't about politics, it was about food.

Fifty years after the Civil War ended and the Americans came to the world's assistance, I renewed my young Vampire feeding practice during the War to End all Wars. During the First World War, I found myself in Europe enjoying the after battle feasts. Trench warfare made after-battle feeding more difficult than the open field/forest battlefields of the Civil War, but not impossible! Some nights I would move through "no-man's land" and sneak into a German trench to dine faster than anyone could see.

It's easy for a Vampire to move (even covertly) more quickly than any blood bag can see. I'd dine late at night and be back in my trench as a soldier long before I would be missed. I always made a point of slicing my meal's throat after dining to make it look like a more natural wartime death! One day we were mowed down by a line of German machine gun entrenches; come sundown we laid in our trenches knowing the next dawn would bring another impossibly deadly day. We were ordered to take the hill and the rear-brass didn't care if it was impossible. After hypnotizing a few of my fellow men-in-arms, who couldn't sleep owing to battle fears, I would slink off and feed among the Germans. After I feasted, I went crazy with my combat knife and wasted as many Germans as I could. With Vampire speed, I was able to dispatch too many to count!

The next day we took the hill to everybody's surprise—to everyone's surprise, but one … the well-fed Vampire.

During World War II, I volunteered to fight in the Pacific for a change of pace from my fighting in Europe during World War I. When the opportunity arose, I was not against sneaking into the jungle brush and making a meal of a lonesome Jap or two. I stopped slicing the throats of my meals. I figured leaving my two pricks in the neck as a calling card would freak out the enemy who believed Vampires to be malevolent ghosts. The Japs tended to stay in groups, if only in small groups and this made meal time a little more challenging, but I usually would eventually find someone alone to dine on. Jap snipers would have been easy prey, if only Vampires really did have the ability to change into a bat and fly up to the top of the trees, a favorite sniper position for Jap snipers. Vampires do not sweat, which was a problem when fighting in the jungle. All the other guys in my unit would sweat up a storm and I'd stay dry. If someone commented on it, I'd just tell them I was from Southern Texas and this jungle heat was nothing to Texas. Some believed me others just looked at me strangely.

It was not long after World War II was won before the next war was being fought. I know the Korean War wasn't a war, but a military police action. Right! Military police action or war, it was a field of feasting for a Vampire.

During this military action I got myself placed on a special infiltration unit whose job it was to go alone into any territory and gather Intel on enemy positions, making notes on their strength and weakness while harassing (or HORRORASSING, as I would like to think of it) the enemy whenever possible. I couldn't think of a better way to harass the enemy than to feed on their blood and leave the drained rotting carcasses to be found by other enemy blood bags.

I was in heaven!

If I were lucky enough to find a Vietcong in the jungle so alone where gunfire would not attract others too quickly, I loved suddenly appearing six to ten feet in front of my next meal. I would let him see me suddenly appear out of nowhere, and let him surge with fear as he emptied his weapon into me without seemingly hurting me! I would walk up to my next meal grinning so that he could see my fangs extracting before plunging them into his neck.

(I would have to fight the temptation to do this too often; it was a bit hard to explain on my arriving back at camp; my being perfectly healthy in my shot up uniform!)

Sometimes I would come across an enemy patrol resting. I just could not help suddenly appearing among them; drop a couple of grenades (pins already pulled) and suddenly disappearing! If I were lucky, one or two would still be alive enough for me to feed on afterwards. Not to brag, but sometimes I'd remove whole enemy camps that way. Those were the days!

During the Vietnam War, I was put in a special infiltration unit again. We went into the jungle for days or weeks at a time, gathering info on the enemy and terrorizing them when possible. Naturally (for a Vampire) I went back to my horrorasing the enemy by feeding on them and leaving their blood-drained carcasses rotting in the jungle to be found by other enemy blood bags! I heard tales of frightened enemy combatant blood bags who, upon surrendering, jabbered in fear about their friends drained of blood. Of course, no one ever took them seriously. I repeat, those were the days!

I have to admit, I enjoyed feeding on the dying during the Civil War (not to mention WWI, WWII, the Korean War, and the Vietnam War) I felt righteous about feeding on the enemy, but I was a very young, naive, improperly trained Vampire at the time. Reading this Vampire Owner's Manual and heeding its words should prevent such improper behavior while feeding.

Vampire Clubs

Vampire clubs tend to look completely different from Vampire bars. The club tends to have fancy lighting, but with darkened areas for feeding. Some clubs have separate rooms for that. Vampire clubs tend to have sexual- or (seemingly) danger-filled staged acts to help set the right atmosphere. Like Vampire bars, Vampire clubs also have a bar or bar room so a jittery blood bag can get a drink or two for settling nerves. Note: If you are a walking blood bag out for the night, just to get drunk, don't bother patronizing either a Vampire bar or club. Bartenders are trained to monitor the drinking of blood bags. After all, who wants to feed from a drunken blood bag? And NO, a Vampire cannot get drunk from feeding off a drunken blood bag. It's just so distasteful.

Vampire clubs are really better designed for fresh feeding because they set up sexually charged atmospheres and, under strong supervision, may be persuaded to set up specially ordered fearful situations for that perfectly seasoned (frightened) meal. These places also tend to have a better class of walking blood bags than Vampire bars. Vampire bars do not require membership fees from the fed upon; Vampire clubs tend to provide a better class meal by the charging of membership fees. The fancier and more elaborate the dining arrangement, the higher the membership fees tend to be.

The club situation provides less of a potluck dinner situation, as well as a better-seasoned meal.

There is nothing, I MEAN NOTHING, like sexually coming while feeding on a properly seasoned meal at the same time. The sensation can be like coming twice at the same time!

This raises the question: why do walking blood bags willingly, if not beguilingly, wish to be fed on? As an ex-blood bag, I can answer that one. It's a real sexual turn on, especially if you are sexually coming while being fed on at the same time. It can be like having two super sexual experiences, one on top of the other—a total mind blowing experience! There is also, among some blood bags, the hope that a Vampire will favor you by turning you. How does this happen? After taking blood from a blood bag, the Vampire then cuts himself/herself open for feeding (sharing) their Vampire blood with the blood bag. This is seldom done. Usually what happens is what happened to me. My

Vampire lover, who will remain nameless, got carried away and lost control in her sexual bliss and took too much blood…

We first met at a small sleazy western saloon on the wrong side of the US/Mexican border that catered to gun hands with money who had to cut-and-run from the north, usually for legal reasons. I didn't consider myself a gun hand, but I was on the run. I was forced to cut-and-run from the great state of Texas when a husband smashed into his own bedroom, blazing gun in hand, and found me in bed with his wife. I didn't have a lot of options: I quickly rolled and reached for my side iron and placed three balls of lead into him while he was still shooting too high into the fancy bed board. Being the brother of the local marshal, it didn't take long before there was paper out on me with a reward for murder "Dead or Alive."

Weeks later, I found myself in this sleazy Mexican saloon when this dark-haired beauty invited me up to her room above the bar. The first time she put the bite on me, she timed it to occur when I was my most sexually vulnerable; it was both shocking and totally amazing! I was instantly hers forever. By the way, it is not true that after being bitten thrice by a Vampire you will turn in to a Vampire.

We continued our sexual sessions for days. Between bouts of sexual bliss, she shared tales of her long life. While she was by no means "an old one" she had been around for hundreds of years. She told me tales of such historic greats as the Roman ruler, Caesar. She told how she tried warning Caesar of the "Ides of March" from something she'd overheard from a distance which human ears could not hear. Of course his response was, "I am Caesar; I am God! Fear not, my lady!" It was her tales of history and famous names that started to open my eyes to what was going on around me. It wasn't until the outbreak of the Civil War that I saw the advantage of taking serious note of what was going on around me historically.

We just couldn't get enough of each other; then it happened. *It* was just like every other time. Just as I was coming, she'd put the bite on me, intensifying my sexual pleasure tenfold, but this time she just kept feeding and feeding! I could feel my heart straining; I knew she was about to kill me and I didn't care! When she did stop, she was shocked to see that she had brought me almost to death's door.

"Listen, my love" she said, worry heavy in her voice, "You're close to death, and it's my fault. You don't have to die. I'm going to cut open my beast. Take my blood and live!"

Too weak to argue, when she placed that beautiful rounded soft flesh to my mouth, I did as I was told and died of total bliss!

Hours later, I awoke, and my Vampire lover explained that in feeding on her blood, and through the sharing of her blood, I was now a Vampire myself. She spent some time giving me limited instruction on being a Living Vampire (Oh yeah, I hadn't died, I had just passed out from the total bliss in the sharing of blood!). Between two Vampires, the sex just wasn't the same, and we soon parted. It was that lone wolf thing I mentioned earlier. Eventually I roamed back north, staying away from Texas. To this day, I stay out of Texas, despite the fact that if there is still a paper out on me, it would probably be in some museum.

Vampires are such lone wolves, researching this "owner's manual" had its difficulties. Most fellow Vampires refused to chat, some got nasty about talking to another Vampire. Some got really nasty about my creation of this instruction manual on Vampires. Some fear it will get into the wrong hands—like the hands of Vampire Hunters!

Getting back to Vampire Clubs

You can tell the difference between a Vampire bar and a Vampire club almost immediately. For the sake of superior clientele, a Vampire club will have better, brighter lighting (at least in the main or meeting rooms). The manager makes a point of getting to know both their Vampire clientele and their human clientele who are there to be food. The manager has the responsibility of matching Vampires and meals that are into fear-seasoned experiences and matching Vampires and meals that are into sexually seasoned experiences. Unlike Vampire bars where the *dining* is mostly a quick meal in a dark corner, in Vampire clubs, most of the *dining* is done in rooms specially decorated for setting the mood for a longer, more enjoyable experience for both the Vampire and its meal.

Some Vampire clubs specialize in sexually flavored dining; some cater to S&M dining for the Vampire with more barbaric dining pleasures under careful supervision. While such S&M clubs are carefully supervised, the occasional overfeeding has been known to happen. Usually the Vampire's membership is revoked and the empty (not to mention dead) blood bag is carefully removed. You might be surprised how many walking blood bags disappear every year, but as a Vampire, you most likely would not be surprised how many walking blood bags disappear every year.

Just a note to you walking blood bags who are members of a Vampire club in hopes of becoming a Vampire—You have a better chance of winning the lottery big time or becoming a picture on a milk carton than being turned in to a Vampire!

CHAPTER TWO
LIVING OR UNDEAD

So you're a Vampire! Are you a Living Vampire or an Undead Vampire? It is vital that you know the difference. If you are a Living Vampire, you can still enjoy a sunny day; if you are an Undead Vampire, the sun will light you up like a struck Lucifer! (Lucifer: Old West term for a wooden matchstick.) Burning to death is one of the most painful ways to die. Every one of your thousands of nerve endings will be screaming in pain. The only difference is that Undead Vampires torch faster because you have very dry, easily flammable bodies. The burning process maybe physiologically less painful for an Undead Vampire if the nerve endings have died during the change to undead.

Living Vampire

A Living Vampire is a walking blood bag who was turned, but not killed. "Turned" is the term for changing a walking blood bag into a Vampire.

How does this come about?

Sharing of Vampire blood: A Vampire takes such a shine to a walking blood bag that, after taking blood from the blood bag, the Vampire then opens a vein and shares his (or her) blood. This is what happened to me, except I was turned because my Vampire lover got carried away and took too much blood. Feeling guilty, she spared my life in the sharing of her blood.

Pros and Cons about being a Living Vampire

Pros:

Immortality

You live forever! Almost. If your human body is killed, you become an Undead Vampire (unless your body is totally destroyed.) If a Living Vampire dies he/she becomes an Undead Vampire and continues to exist.

Be warned, your immortality is not the immortality of the gods. I was told a story about a newly created Vampire who mistook immortality with invisibility and felt no concern for Vampire Hunters. Living the life of Vampires he'd seen in movies, he started feeding on blood bags to the point of killing them. This eventually got the attention of a Vampire Hunter that killed the young naive Living Vampire, then out of spite waited until the Vampire was reborn as an Undead Vampire and torched him into non-existence!

Weight Problem

If you had a weight problem as a walking blood bag, you are about to have one less problem. Have you ever seen a fat Vampire? This is impossible on a red fluid protein diet! You can gorge yourself until you feel like a blotted tick, and your body will show no weight gain. No more having to decide what to eat. While you can still eat food, you need the added red protein (blood) to supplement your Vampire digestion system. While your circulatory system is not as sluggish as an Undead Vampire, you still need to regenerate your blood with an external source. If you have a weight problem just go with the blood diet and watch the weight disappear. Just remember—you do not have to kill to enjoy a blood diet.

Sterility

Vamps: A female Living Vampire cannot get pregnant. Gal, if you're a player, this gives you something less to worry about.

Vampires: From my interviews I get the impression that a Living Vampire is less probable to get a female blood bag pregnant, but it can happen. The resulting newborn will not be a Living Vampire.

Personally, I do not believe I have any bastards running around, while I have had a very active sex life. Being a traveler how would I know? I have been known to pop up at places I have traveled before, especially if "Lady Luck" was good at that location. I have never seen anyone in my travels that remotely look like me.

Rapid Healing (Rejuvenation)

Living Vampires heal quickly from all injuries except burning. (If a Vampire gets burned by fire or sun exposure, it takes a long time to heal. If ever!) Injuries received from other Vampires seem to take longer to heal than self-inflicted injuries (accidental) or injuries from blood bags. I know of slower healing from first hand (or face) from attacks by other Vampires. My face learned the hard way that some female Vampires do not like being called "Vamps." Also some Vampires took painful offence to my writing of this *Vampire Owner's Manual.*

Superb Night Vision

If you are a night person (as a Living or Undead Vampire), you will love the hyper-sharp night sight. As a Living Vampire, you may change to a more nighttime lifestyle just because of the advanced night vision. You will particularly enjoy the superb night vision if you hunt in the wild by night for your blood meals. Just remember, there are other creatures of the night that do not attract the attention of a Vampire Hunter. Hunt wild creatures, and no one will take notice. Hunt humans and you are asking for trouble.

Superb Hearing

Do you wonder what the girl across the room is saying? Tune your hearing her way and hear for yourself (and hope you're not sorry for eavesdropping). This can be advantageous if you are the adventurous type and like hunting for your meal in the wild.

Superior Strength

You will suddenly discover that you have the strength of ten men! With your superior strength, you might start getting visions of becoming a super hero... Before you start donning tights and a cape, remember that as a Vampire you want to live low key. Vampire Hunters are out there, and you do not want to attract their attention.

Mind Control

With Vampire maturity, you can hypnotize blood bags to do your will. This is called "enthrallment". You should train with animals first, then advance to more mentally superior walking blood bags. Mind manipulating takes time and training. If you go directly to trying to enthrall a blood bag, you are just asking for an embarrassing moment.

I had been a Vampire for about a hundred years before I learned that a Vampire can enthrall blood bags. If you are a new Vampire, this is a good reason for reading this manual.

As I was saying: I was outside my first Vampire bar and was getting up the nerve to go in when I took notice that a Vampire was being refused entrance. Why? I did not know at the time. In hindsight it most likely had something to do with what followed: I decided to follow this Vampire, instead of entering the Vampire bar.

Some blocks away, I watched this Vampire walk up to a blood bag. He moved in close, eye-to-eye close, and as the blood bag noticeably went limp in his arms, the Vampire fed. He did not stop feeding until the blood bag's life was extinguished. Later, in conversation with a fellow Vampire, I learned of the gift of enthrallment.

Intense Sexual Pleasure

Time your blood feeding during orgasms and you may never feed differently again. Put the bite on your meal just as you're coming and it will be like coming two-fold. Put the bite on your meal as they're coming and they're yours forever (or until you make the mistake of turning them). If you have read the "Introduction," you know I speak from experience.

Burning the Candle at Both Ends

As a Living Vampire, you can go days without sleeping (unlike an Undead Vampi re who needs to return to his or her coffin nightly). This means you can continue your day life and party by night, every night for a week or more with Vampire maturity!

Personally, I have to be careful not to ever tax "Lady Luck" and gamble for days at a time and raise curiosity as to how I can gamble for such an unnatural amount of time without sleep.

Cons:

Feeding
You can still eat like a blood bag, but you're not going to want to except for the purpose of a lifestyle disguise. You can still eat food and digest food, but everything basically tastes like cardboard. Remember: Blood is the life, not pizza!

Heightened Vision
Get yourself a good pair of shades; you're going to need them. Until you mature some, you'll even need them indoors as well as outdoors. In some civilizations wearing shades even at night … *is cool*, and totally acceptable.

I found fellow gamblers had a problem playing with a fellow gambler who wore shades at the table. For a while, I made a point of only gambling at night and in darkened areas of the establishment.

Superb Hearing
If you are a concert goer, get yourself some earplugs, because with your heightened hearing you're not going to be able to stand loud noises easily. Of course, you could now enjoy the concert without paying for a ticket, if you don't mind enjoying the concert from a mile away!

Increased Strength
You will suddenly discover you have the strength of ten men. You're superior to walking blood bags, but you have to constantly remember to hide your abilities, so you won't attract the attention of Vampire Hunters—what a bummer!

While visiting an unnamed big city, I came across a scene where a gang of hoods was messing with a young lady. Despite the fact that she looked dressed for trouble, in her skimpy leather skirt and tube top, she looked to be in trouble. I interfered...

"Excuse me, please. I appear to be lost."

"You sure are, dude!" the one still holding a knife in front of the young lady said. "I suggest you boogie while you still can!"

"Fine. This lady and I will just be leaving together..."

"You will over my dead body!" He lunged at me with a knife leading his attack.

I simply moved to the side, leaving one foot in place, outstretched. The knife wielder fell over my foot. As he passed by, I gave him a chop behind the neck that either knocked him out or broke his neck. I really did not care which. Another hood charged me with a chain swinging for my head. I put an arm up and let the chain wrap harmlessly around it. I then pulled the hood toward me and chopped him in the neck. He dropped like a dead log—possibly because he was now as dead as a log. I looked in the direction of another attacker, this one with a knife that looked bigger and nastier than the first knife. I side-stepped as I did the first attacker. Only this attacker was prepared for that and swung his deadly knife with the goal of splitting my chest in two. Jumping back and out of the deadly ark of the knife, the attack failed. I stepped in and grabbed his wrist, trapping his arm in a viselike grip between us. I slowly, purposely, squeezed his wrist until it audibly snapped, and the hood crumpled in pain, dropping the knife. Shoving the hood to the ground I nonchalantly kicked the knife too far away to see where it went.

Looking around, there was only the girl in the outfit that said "I'm looking for trouble" and one more hood. This hood stood frozen, just staring at me. I said, "Boo!," and the hood did a disappearing act. He failed to disappear before I smelled the wet spot growing on his pants.

"Madam, may I escort you somewhere?"

Shakily, she answered, "Yes...I just live three blocks away."

So I made a show of taking her arm and walking her in the direction she indicated with her eyes. We got two blocks when a police car drove past, and the lady on my arm screamed, "POLICE!"

I will not bother you with the rest of the night's activities, except that it was a busy night with police and reporters (that I was able to avoid).

The next night I spotted two Vampire Hunters in the area (presumably because of the news articles about the night before). I had to leave before I planned to…all because I came to the aid of a woman who meant nothing to me.

Moral of the story: Keep low key or face the Vampire Hunters.

Morphing

Normally, you cannot change into animals (like you may have seen in the movies); there may be exceptions for Vampires who have received their gift through magic or from the devil. Remember: you can learn to control animals. Given time, you can control large packs of animals from dogs, to wolves, and from large packs of rats to bats. This mental control of animals may be where the belief in Vampires changing into animals came from.

Heightened Sense of Smell

If you're the he-man type who likes to hang out and work out in gyms—FORGET IT! The intensified stench of sweating bodies will just be too much, not to mention the intense smell of food in the form of sweating blood bags.

Beware of highly seasoned foods; their odor can be a little overwhelming at times.

Undead Vampire

An Undead Vampire is a Vampire who was a living blood bag or a Living Vampire who has died.

How does this happen?

Sharing of Vampire Blood

A Vampire takes such a shine to a walking blood bag that, after taking blood from the blood bag, the Vampire then opens a vein and shares his (or her) blood. If the Vampire takes too much blood from the walking blood bag, he or she will die of blood loss anyway.

Cannibalism

Definition:

1: the usually ritualistic eating of human flesh by a human being

2: the eating of the flesh of an animal by another animal of the same kind
3: an act of cannibalizing something [Merriam-Webster]

To a Vampire, a cannibal is a walking blood bag who has eaten the flesh and drunk the blood of other blood bags. At death, sometimes a cannibal rises from the dead as an Undead Vampire. It's unclear why all cannibals don't rise as such, but the general census is that cannibals who have lived that lifestyle don't become Undead Vampires, but normal blood bags who take on cannibalistic ways late in life can arise as Undead Vampires.

Consumption of Blood

Consumption of blood by a walking blood bag is not the same as cannibalism, but it can be assumed some consumption of blood is inevitable during cannibalistic consumption.

As seen above, a cannibal is a human who has consumed the flesh of the living. This may explain why walking blood bags who take on cannibalism become Undead Vampires. During cannibalism, a human consumes blood while eating flesh and could become an Undead Vampire at death. The Holy Bible even warns about this in the 12th chapter of Deuteronomy.

Change of Faith

Supposedly, if you denounce your Orthodox faith, and declare allegiance to another faith, at death your dead body will not rest, and you will rise as an Undead Vampire. I have not personally seen such an Undead Vampire, but Undead Vampires tend to be even more difficult to chat with than Living Vampires.

Bane of Vampire Hunters

I have talked to two Undead Vampires who were Vampire Hunters in life! What a colossal joke. You spend your whole life in the noble pursuit of killing demon Vampires, and then at your death you rise up and become the target of other Vampire Hunters.

It has been surmised that during years of killing Vampires, a Vampire Hunter gets Vampire blood on them. Some of this blood can't help but be absorbed into the Hunter's skin, then mix with his blood.

Then at the death of this holier-than-thou Vampire Hunter, the tainted blood causes the ex-hunter to become the hunted.

Pros and Cons of the Undead Vampire
Pros:

Immortality
You're not dead—you're undead! You can still continue continuing on. (Just remember: Only at night).

Morphing
Changing into mist (not an ability of a Living Vampire): a ghostly Undead Vampire can change into a mist that can slip through cracks. Becoming a mist creature, you can fly by drifting with the wind. Just be careful of windy weather. I heard of a Vampire in mist form who got blown away!

Rapid Healing
While an Undead Vampire heals rapidly from injuries compared to blood bags, I'm told Undead Vampires heal more slowly than Living Vampires. Most likely, this has to do with the sluggish nearly dead anatomy of an Undead Vampire. While Living Vampires can heal from burns, an Undead Vampire will not heal from a burn of any degree.

Sterility
An Undead Vampire is physically mostly dead. Neither a female nor a male Vampire can produce sexually. Female Vampires (or "Vamps") can't have children. They do have the advantage over male Vampires as they can at least fake it for sexually arousing their planned dinner. While male Living Vampires can get a blood bag pregnant, a male Undead Vampire not only can't get a female pregnant, he can't even get it up to fake it!

Mind Control
It does appear that Undead Vampires have more mental control of animals than Living Vampires do. This does not follow with mental

control of walking blood bags. While as an Undead Vampire you do still have mental control of walking blood bags, being undead doesn't increase your powers compared to a Living Vampire.

I was told of a story where a couple was spending the closing daylight hours visiting a deceased loved one at a cemetery. A resting Undead Vampire heard them close by. As it was still daylight he could not take immediate advantage of their presence, so he used his advanced mind control to bring every wild dog in the area to close in on the couple. With the falling of the sun, the Undead Vampire misted out from his coffin and was able to dine on the couple he found properly trapped by the enthralled pack of dogs.

Cons:

Living by Day

No more living by day! You're undead; you're a creature of the night—get over it! As an Undead Vampire, you must return to your coffin before daybreak. If you fail to return to your coffin by the break of dawn, you're toast. As the skyline lightens, you will start feeling uncomfortably hot. As the sun comes near to its horizon you will feel extremely hot. As the sun breaks the horizon and the rays of light strike you, you will ignite like a struck Lucifer!

A NOTE OF WARNING: Give careful consideration to your place of rest! Many Undead Vampires have awakened to their new un-life to find that their coffin has been buried within a graveyard. Soon after, they discover the ease of misting out of the coffin and through the ground. Eventually, they consider their new gravesite to be a great place to hide their coffin—WRONG!

Any Vampire Hunter worth a grain of salt will visit the local graveyards with a horse in tow, looking for Vampires in hiding. Horses have a keen sense for potential predators and will not walk over a grave containing a Vampire. Hunters walk the horses over the graveyard by day (of course), so if the horse fails to walk over a grave, the Vampire Hunter simply digs up the coffin, opens it up to sunlight, and steps back while the Vampire is totally ignited like a camera's flashbulb.

Remember that Undead Vampire who held a couple in reach with a pack of enthralled dogs? He failed to remove the remains of his meal. Despite the damage to the remains, the story of the couple killed by dogs caught the interest of a Vampire Hunter. He found the Undead Vampire's grave with a rented horse, and when the horse failed to walk over the grave, the Vampire Hunter dug up the coffin. With the sun still high in the sky, he opened the coffin and stood by to watch the Undead Vampire detonated like a flammable explosive.

Sunlight

As mentioned above, sunlight will light up an Undead Vampire like a struck Lucifer. Undead Vampire skin is extremely dry, and highly flammable. The Undead Vampire body is a very deadly dry-skinned body that will torch extremely fast to sunlight.

Slower Healing

While an Undead Vampire heals much faster than a blood bag, an Undead Vampire heals slower than a Living Vampire. While a Living Vampire will heal from burns from fire or sun, Undead Vampires will not! Remember: Undead Vampires don't even survive sunlight, let alone heal from sunburns (unlike what you may see in moving pictures). You cannot lather sunscreen on heavily and go out into the sunlight. You cannot go out into the sun by covering yourself up. You'll live a little longer, if you call quickly dehydrating to the point of steaming to death living longer!

Complexion

It is harder for Undead Vampires to pass themselves off as walking blood bags because of the death-like complexion that comes with existing only by night. It's not like you can use a tanning bed to get a living look to your complexion. A tanning bed would be a great way to commit suicide! Given time, your nightlife will cause your eye pupils to turn red. Between the light complexion and the red eyes, you might get away with telling blood bags that you are an albino.

Dry Skin

Vamps, you thought you had a dry skin problem as a walking blood bag! Wait until you become one of the undead! I have heard of Vamps who have committed suicide over their dry skin problem.

Sterility

Vamps: Female Vampires can't have children. This could be a real con depending on surviving interest in motherhood.

Vampires: Male Vampires cannot get a female (Vamp or walking blood bag) pregnant. In fact, your tool is dead; you can't even get it up.

Diet

As an undead Vampire, your diet is a total Red Protein Diet. A Living Vampire can still eat, mostly for the purpose of lifestyle disguise. However, as an Undead Vampire, your digestion system is totally dead. You can't digest food. If you try eating food, it will just come right back up! This means your blood can no longer regenerate itself. You need to regenerate by outside sources such as feeding. As an Undead Vampire, there is a greater necessity for blood feeding than as a Living Vampire, as you need this crimson fluid of life more often than a Living Vampire would.

While you cannot starve to a point of non-existence, you can starve to the point of immense pain and weakness. If you continue to starve yourself, you will weaken to the point of not being able to feed yourself. The result is a constant cycle of starvation, pain and weakness that you will not be able to break without someone's help. From what I have found in my research, you will wish for death, but it will not happen. I shiver at the thought of this being used as a form of torture for a Vampire.

Heightened Sensitivity

You're going to find yourself wearing shades a lot because of visual sensitivity. If you're one for going to concerts, you're either going to have to change your lifestyle or get used to earplugs; your new sensitive hearing will not stand the loud noise!

If you were a Living Vampire before becoming an Undead Vampire, your olfactory system will still be hypersensitive. If you have changed into an Undead Vampire directly from a blood bag, and were never a Living Vampire, you will have to fight the impulse of overfeeding on a blood bag to the point of their death as an overreaction to the smell of their blood.

Lack of Reflection

A lack of the ability to use a mirror. Yes, it's true. Undead Vampires can't see themselves in mirrors! It's still unclear why an Undead Vampire can form themselves well enough to be seen by others, but cannot form themselves enough to make a reflection on any shiny surface. But I can say that it has nothing to do with Undead Vampires being pure evil. While Undead Vampires tend to be less social than Living Vampires, not all Undead Vampires are pure evil! Beware of cameras: Undead Vampires cannot be photographed. You will either not appear in the photo at all, or you might appear in the photo as a fine mist. Either result is a bit hard to explain to blood bags. You can't see your face in a mirror, but as an Undead Vampire, your hair is still growing, and you still need to shave. This makes shaving more difficult, but not impossible.

Travelling

Traveling as an Undead Vampire can be much more difficult since you have to return to your coffin every morning! An Undead Vampire can get around this by packing boxes of earth from the burial ground, but do I have to tell you how difficult Bram Stoker's Dracula has made doing so!

Vampire Pets

If you were a pet lover or owner while alive as a blood bag or Living Vampire and still wish to have a pet, forget about it! Once you become one of the Undead Vampires, your "pet" will have nothing to do with you. If you try to force your love on your pet canine or feline, it will only try to fight or flee from you out of fear for its life. It will not see you as its loving master anymore.

So you figure, 'Okay, there's a solution to this: I will just 'turn' my loving pet into a vampire pet and all will be right as virgin blood. Wrong!

Turn your pet into a Vampire pet and it will, without fail, turn on you with twice the ferocity it ever showed when still living: This time with no hesitation and without any fear. There is no such thing as a Vampire pet!

Once you 'turn' that which so loved you when you both were alive, you have now created a bloodthirsty killing machine that will attack anyone or anything for food, including other Vampires, and especially its previous master. While your pet is still living, you can enthrall it to your will. Controlling through enthrallment what once was your loving pet is not the same as when you were alive and had a equally nurturing relationship. An enthralled animal does not have your pet's same love and devotion.

I have heard repeatedly that these attempts lead to frustration and a bad end of the once loving pet. Once I was turned and was ready to hit the trail again, I witnessed this first hand with my horse, Dusty. No amount of tender words or feeding was going to get Dusty to be my trusted travelling companion again. In fact, when I tried to feed him, he refused to eat. The stable hand had to feed him to keep the horse from starving to death.

Not wanting to hurt Dusty, I tried turning another horse to see if this would solve the problem. It didn't. The horse tried to stomp and bite me to death. Having a true spark of the devil in its eyes, I felt I had no choice but to put the animal down. First I tried shooting it in the chest. That just made it meaner. Then I tried to put it down with a shot to the head. If it was possible, I made it even meaner. Remember, I was a young basically untrained Vampire.

Eventually, I came up with the idea: I would burn down the stables with the demon horse trapped inside. For an ungodly time this demon horse screamed a scream that could only come from hell itself, but at some point as the structure finished burning to the ground, so ended the existence of this demon beast from hell.

I left Dusty in the care of the stable hand who now had to corral Dusty and the other horses outside until a new stable could be built. Why did I not try to enthrall Dusty to my will? I was too young and inexperienced to know about the ability of mentally forcing the living to my will.

Eventually, I did take to occasionally enthralling a horse to my will for temporary travel needs. Afterward, I would either let the beast go or have it for dinner. Mostly I started travelling by stagecoach or train, then years later by iron horses, later cars, buses and trucks. Just remember: there is no such thing as a Vampire pet!

"The Old Ones"

A note on "the Old Ones:" These are extremely old Vampires who are almost deified by all other Vampires, Living and Undead alike. Since no one knows where the first Vampire came from, no one can even decide if an Old One is a Living or Undead Vampire. (Vampires are so awed by "the Old Ones" that it is hard to get a Vampire of any age to even speak of them.) All the Old Ones have matured their abilities to an amazing degree, almost making them demigods!

Here is a most intriguing folktale on the first Old One: *Genesis' Adam and Eve*—as the tale goes, Eve was not Adam's first wife. A real bitch named Lilith was the first. She was created from the same soil as Adam, hence she considered herself equal to Adam.

Lilith was such a bitch that God threw her out of Eden and started all over again with Eve. Lilith started eating animals before God gave permission for humans to do so, and on her death, Lilith became the first Vampire! By the time Lilith was reborn as a Vampire, Adam and Eve had spawned many generations of walking blood bags, due to a much longer life span compared to today.

Some ancient writings have God banishing Lilith after destroying all her children in front of her, so when Lilith was reborn as a Vampire, she took out her vengeance by feeding on the children of Adam and Eve. This explains why Vampires crave blood from humans instead of animals.

You can find this tale in ancient Jewish writings as well as in many cult literatures.

CHAPTER THREE
ILLNESSES THAT MIMIC VAMPIRISM

Below are some illnesses that have been suspected of creating Vampires or creating Vampire lore. These are blood illness that, before recent modern treatments, may have caused victims to attack blood bags at night for their blood. (One paper I read suggested that the illness below could have brought about some cases of cannibalism or created some ghouls.)

Porphyria

Porphyria is a rare hereditary blood disease preventing a victim from producing heme (an oxygen carrier), a major and vital component of red blood cells.

Vampire-mimicking symptoms are:

*Extreme sensitivity to sunlight

*Deformities of the face, especially the skull, causing a death-like appearance.

*Tightening of skin and gums (which could make the incisors more prominent, giving the mouth a fang-like appearance.)

*Excessive hair growth

*Aversion to garlic

A person with porphyria must avoid sunlight because it causes changes in their heme, a component of blood that carries oxygen throughout the body and is used to remove carbon dioxide. In sunlight, their heme is turned into a toxic substance, which the body then tries to break down. Lacking the ability to dispose of these toxic substances, the body deposits them on the skin, gums, and teeth. As the disease grows worse, the skin blackens, swells, and ruptures. Someone suffering with such a disease would only come out at night. Over time, the victim would take on an unnaturally scary look, fangs and all.

Such a victim would suffer painfully for fresh blood due to the malfunctioning heme. Such a person may take to stealing the blood of others to exist—like Vampires.

According to Vampire lore, Vampires can't see their reflections in mirrors. This may have come about from porphyria suffers who would find their reflections extremely disturbing.

Porphyria sufferers might be further mistaken for Vampires because of their avoidance of garlic. It was a well-known way to keep Vampires at bay. Garlic contains chemicals that are believed to exacerbate porphyria's symptoms. These chemicals can cause an agonizing attack in even a mild case of the disease.

Medical examinations of thousands of Vampires during trials and convictions in the 17th century have the medical profession believing that possibly as many as 600 convicted "Vampires" were cases of porphyria.

Lupus

Lupus is a chronic, inflammatory autoimmune disease caused by multiple genetic, environmental and other factors, some unknown to date. This is a very complicated disease that may appear a thousand different ways in a thousand different people. The Lupus Foundation of America estimates that approximately 1,400,000 Americans have a form of Lupus. The difficulty with Lupus is that it differs greatly case by case. The disease has a long list of symptoms, and attacks a wide variety of tissues—especially the skin, joints, blood, and kidneys.

Lupus occurs when a person's own B cells produce antibodies that are directed against good body tissue. These antibodies—secreted proteins also called "hemoglobins" or "heme" that help the body clear infections—normally target foreign pathogens in the bloodstream or inside infected cells. In Lupus, the antibodies target the body's own molecules instead.

For instance, many people who have Lupus produce an antibody that targets red blood cells, which are vital oxygen-transporting components of blood. The antibodies attack the red blood cells by surrounding or "coating" them. These coated cells are then taken up and destroyed by macrophages. Macrophages (Greek for big eaters) are the defense mechanism for getting rid of dangerous or harmful cells, such as disease producers. This can lead to a deficiency of red blood cells and anemia (lack of oxygen within the body system).

Lupus has a long list of symptoms, some of which could mimic vampirism. Below are a few of those Vampire-like symptoms:

* Sensitivity to sunlight: Sunlight causes some Lupus victims great pain and may easily cause dangerous, damaging sunburns.
* Anemia: Lack of heme in the bloodstream.
* Pale skin tone: Years of illness and lack of sunlight could cause a deathly pale skin tone.

A victim of Lupus would seem very Vampire-like. Such a person suffering from photosensitivity or sensitivity to sunlight would only go out at night and would eventually develop a Vampire's pale skin tone. If a Lupus sufferer is a victim of anemia, he or she might start craving blood, even to the point of stealing it from others.

I had a meal with a couple at a Vampire club who told me they had a child at home with Lupus. This child had to be home-schooled because she could not go out during the day and could not go to school at night; her photosensitivity included sensitivity to florescent lights, which are used primarily in schools. Outside the family, the child had no friends because years of illness had given her a "scary" look. She had pale skin tone with tight-drawn skin that gave her both a skeleton-like look to the head as well as making her teeth more prominent, almost looking like fangs. This young victim of Lupus seldom goes out at night for fear someone will see her, point at her and scream, "Vampire!"

Rabies

Rabies is a viral disease that causes acute inflammation of the brain in warm-blooded animals. The incubation period of the rabies virus in humans averages from two to eight weeks, but may vary from ten days to ten months, or more, depending on the location of the bite, the severity of the wound, and its proximity to the central nervous system. The symptoms of the disease in humans are relevant to our discussion. These, according to modern clinical observations, include: hyperactivity, disorientation, hallucinations, seizures, bizarre behavior, and stiffness or paralysis of the neck. In most cases, a period of marked hyperactivity (furious rabies) develops, lasting hours to days. The hyperactivity consists of periods of agitation, thrashing, running, biting, or other bizarre behavior. These episodes may occur spontaneously or may be precipitated by tactile, auditory, visual, or olfactory stimuli.

Historically, before the 15th century, rabies cases were rare, but during the 15th and 16th centuries, there was a massive outbreak of rabies throughout Europe. During this same time, there was also a massive outbreak of Vampire trials going on throughout Europe.

*Symptoms that mimic Vampirism:
*Hypersensitivity to garlic
*Hypersensitivity to sunlight (or light in general)
*Narcolepsy: Sleeping by day.

A person starts showing Vampire-like signs (see above) and then (if not treated) the victim dies … to complete the change to Vampire.

It doesn't help that rabies may come from animals associated with Vampires, like wolves, bats and rats!

Rabies May Have Inspired Vampire Legend

NEW YORK, September 21 (Reuters)—Mistaken for blood-thirsty ghouls, 18th century European rabies victims may have been the inspiration for the Vampire legend, according to a report in the September issue of the Journal Neurology.

Not only do people with rabies have symptoms strikingly similar to the traits ascribed to Vampires, but the Vampire legend also originated in eastern Europe in the 18th century—the site of a major rabies outbreak in the 1720s, according to the study.

Rabies, a virus usually transmitted via the bite of an infected animal, can be tricky to diagnose, the study's author, Dr. Juan Gomez-Alonso told Reuters Health in an interview. Symptoms usually do not appear for at least a couple of weeks, and by then the bite has healed. Once symptoms have appeared, anti-rabies treatment is ineffective, and the infection is most often fatal.

"Even now we miss diagnoses in cases of rabies," Gomez-Alonso said. Citing an example in his study, Gomez-Alonso describes a relatively recent case in which a man presumed to be a "wandering lunatic" was found to be infected with rabies during an autopsy. "These missed diagnoses probably happened much more commonly in the 18th century," Gomez-Alonso added.

A neurologist at Hospital Xeral in Vigo, Spain, Gomez-Alonso decided to investigate the rabies-vampirism connection after watching a Vampire movie in 1981.

"I had never seen a Vampire movie before and I was struck by the similarities," he explained.

There are many cases of rabies, Gomez-Alonso reports in the study. For starters, not only people, but also dogs, wolves, and bats—animals traditionally associated with Vampires—can be infected with the rabies virus. Because the virus affects the limbic system, the part of the brain that influences aggressive and sexual behavior, people with rabies tend to be aggressive, may attempt to bite others, and are "hypersexual," he writes. Since rabies also affects the hypothalamus, the part of the brain that controls sleep, many patients suffer from insomnia, and are up and about in the middle of the night.

Rabies causes hypersensitivity to strong stimuli, as well, so patients are often repelled by light, by bright things such as mirrors, and by strong odors, including the smell of garlic. Rabies victims may vomit blood, Gomez-Alonso explains, and since the disease causes hydrophobia, or aversion to water, they do not swallow their saliva, which can froth at their mouths, flecked with blood.

The disease can also cause facial spasms, in which the lips jerk back over the teeth, in an animal-like snarl. Moreover, rabies is more common among men than women, as is vampirism, at least according to most Vampire tales. Finally, rabies, like vampirism, can be transmitted via a bite, Gomez-Alonso writes. The infection, however, can also be transmitted via a scratch or across mucus membranes. Consequently, it can be contracted during sex with an infected partner, or by inhaling air in caves heavily populated by infected bats.

In addition to the medical evidence, Gomez-Alonso provides historical support for his theory. Digging through centuries-old European archives, he found records of a rabies epidemic among dogs, wolves and other animals in Hungary between 1721 and 1728, the time people first began to report sightings of "Vampires." There were reports, for instance, of people "who have been dead for several years, or at least several months and seen to return, to talk, to walk, to infest the villages and to suck the blood of their close ones, making them become ill and eventually die. "

Gomez-Alonso also found accounts of bodies, exhumed after burial, that appeared life-like, and were filled with still-liquid blood. This also fits in with the rabies theory, he writes. When people die of collapse, shock, or asphyxiation—as is often the case with rabies—their blood is often slow to clot. Moreover, the region of Hungary where the outbreak occurred is damp and cold many months of the year, significant because corpses take longer to decompose in the cold. "Their good appearance would also suggest the presence of saponification," he explains. "This process, characteristic of burials in humid places, transforms the subcutaneous tissues into a wax-like substance."

"Much evidence supports that rabies could have played a key role in the generation of the Vampire legend," later popularized in Bram Stoker's "Dracula" and numerous other books and films, Gomez-Alonso concludes. "This would be in accordance with the anthropologic theory that assumes that many popular legends have been prompted by facts. Under this approach, saying that the Vampire is 'mere fiction' may be somewhat inappropriate. "

SOURCE: Neurology 1998;51:856-859.

Photosensitivity
Photosensitivity is sensitivity to sunlight (or even florescent light) to the point of physical damage. Usually this is not a disease by itself, but a

symptom of a worse disease. Photosensitivity in its severest form can cause severe pain, loss of eyesight; loss of fingers and toes and/or death.

Anemia

The word "anemia" is derived from the Greek word for "bloodlessness." Anemia is a blood disease in which the red blood cell count is usually low. Red blood cells are the carriers of oxygen throughout the body (heme). When a person suffers from anemia, their symptoms are caused by inadequate oxygen. Anemia is more often a symptom of a greater disease than a disease itself.

Symptoms that mimic Vampirism
    *Pale complexion
    *Daytime fatigue
    *Digestive disorders

Tuberculosis

Pre-Civil War, this highly contagious disease went by the name "consumption". Once one member of a family died from it, other family members would follow in time, giving the impression that the newly dead was coming back as a Vampire and consuming the living members of the family. Even worse, when the deceased member of the family was exhumed, they would appear bloated, as one who just freshly fed on blood. The normal development of gas within a decaying body was not known back then.

Symptoms that mimic Vampirism
    *Red, swollen eyes (which also creates a sensitivity to bright light)
    *Pale skin
    *Extremely low body heat
    *Weak heart
    *Coughing up blood (It is said that this coughing up of blood created fear in some people; seeing this would create fear that there would be blood attacks to replace what was being coughed up.)
    Today tuberculosis can be treated with antibiotics; but it is still a difficult illness to treat and from which to recover.

Mental Illness

With the popularity of Vampirism in books and moving pictures, I can't help but wonder: Among the many Napoleons, Caesars and George Washingtons in any given insane asylum, how many Vampires are in there?!

Premature Burial

In the years preceding modern medicine, there are historic accounts of people prematurely buried, assumed dead. Later, the person would make sounds while reviving that could be heard coming from the coffin … possibly Vampires?

In some cases, the person would bang his/her face against the coffin, making his/her face bloody such that when the coffin was opened, the person would look like a feeding Vampire. Such a person would be staked and put to rest, really dead this time.

Up to the 18th century, some coffins were designed with a string inside the coffin that would lead to a bell outside of the coffin, in case the newly deceased was prematurely buried and needed to ring the bell to get out.

So you think you're a Vampire. Before you embrace your new lifestyle maybe you should see a doctor … or a shrink!

CHAPTER FOUR
BASIC VAMPIRISM

In the Oxford dictionary the word "Vampire" means "a ghost that leaves his grave at night and sucks the blood of sleeping people".

Most people who think of Vampires think of Europe, but ancient Greece and Rome had Vampires long before the Hungarians. In Greece, they were called "lamiae," and in Rome, they were "striges" or "lamiae." In fact, there are tales of Vampires all through history and all around the globe. [See CHAPTER 10: VAMPIRES AROUND THE WORLD]

It's not hard to see how the myth of vampirism became so deeply rooted in Romania and Transylvania. The people were Greek Orthodox in religion, as was Dracula. The orthodox doctrine states, "Anyone bound by a curse will not be received by the Earth and will not decay."

Anyone who is cataloged as a cannibal, bloodsucker, or one who gives up his Orthodox faith is also considered cursed. The real historical Dracula did. He drank blood, ate human flesh, and gave up his Orthodox faith as part of terms for release from prison. To the Orthodox, such a curse does not make you a Vampire but a morai (undead). A Vampire is an undead bloodsucker or bloodsucking morai. The belief in Vampires is still strong in "Dracula country" today.

In 1969, a gypsy named Tinka who lived near Castle Dracula told two authors these two stories:

1) When her father died, he was laid out promptly and the next day he was found still full of signs of life despite the fact that he had no heartbeat. The villagers knew he was undead and put a spike in his heart.

2) An old woman died in the village. After many of her close relatives, and the animals around her house were found killed, the villagers opened the old woman's grave and found her eyes open. Furthermore, she had rolled over in her coffin. Her face still showed signs of life. The villagers burned her corpse.

In 1923, the English outlawed the practice of putting stakes through people who had committed suicide.

Some Asian Beliefs
In India, there are ancient writings about the Vetala, a ghoulish creature that can sometimes be found hanging upside down from tree branches in graveyards. These bloodsuckers were evildoers or insane when alive.

India even had Vampiric gods such as Kali, who wore the heads of her victims as a necklace around her neck.

Kali are beautiful women by day who transform by night into horrid bloodsuckers with insect-like elongated proboscis-like tongues and huge bat-like wings.

Some Asian Vampires specialize in attacking pregnant women as they sleep to suck out the life of the unborn. (Interesting way to explain away a still-born infant: "The Manananggal (Vampire) did it!")

Vampires sometimes strike people dumb. They can steal your beauty or your strength.

Some Romanian Beliefs
One of the most common ways of locating a Vampire was to choose a boy or girl, young enough to be a virgin, and seat him or her upon a virgin horse that is solid colored, and has never stumbled. The horse is led through the cemetery and over all the graves. If the horse refuses to pass over a grave, a Vampire is thought to lie there. (This belief is overstated. I grew up on a farm and have worked with horses. I can tell you that any horse worth its feed has an intense sense for a dangerous predator, like a Vampire asleep in its coffin, and will refuse to walk over it! No special horse or requirements are necessary.)

Usually the tomb of a Vampire has one or more holes roughly the size through which a serpent or mist can pass.

Crosses made from the thorns of wild roses are effective in keeping the Vampire away. Making a cross in tar on your front door should keep Vampires out, as will smearing certain herbal plants around your doors and windows, depending on the Vampire you are trying to keep out.

When you find a Vampire's coffin, there are numerous ways to kill it within the coffin:

1) Hammer a stake through the heart. This stops the flow of stolen blood and seems to kill the Vampire, but if someone removes the stake, the heart will regenerate, and the vampire will awaken and come out from within the coffin.

2) Place the body under running water. This forces the Vampire to stay with its coffin, but if the coffin is removed from under the water the Vampire is released from its coffin.

3) Shoot a Vampire with a silver bullet, blessed by a priest. This will have the same results as a wooden stake in the heart, but if the bullet is removed, it is the same as removing said wooden stake.

4) Cut off the head and insert stakes into the heart and leg muscles. This is one better than the stake in the heart, but if the stake is removed from the heart with the Vampire head in near proximity, then as the heart regenerates, so will the connection of the head to the body.

(For Undead Vampires…)

5) When the Vampire is away, burn its coffin. This is a really good way to eliminate the problem if the Vampire is an Undead Vampire and needs to return to its coffin each night.

6) Trick the Vampire into the light, and it will decay. This is a given IF the Vampire is an Undead Vampire

7) The best way: Stake the Vampire (Living or Undead) in the heart to immobilize it. Decapitate the head from the body. Then prepare two fires some distance apart and burn the head in one and the coffined body in the second fire. Bury the ashes in two different places. This procedure is basically foolproof. Note: The two fires are not required if the Vampire is Undead, then you can just wait for the rising of the sun.

Misconceptions

Let's end some misconceptions right now …

As a Vampire, you have to return to your coffin before sunrise to sleep—Wrong. This is only if you are an Undead Vampire. If you are a Living Vampire, there is no change required in your sleeping habit.

Vampires can't cross running water—Wrong: If you are an Undead Vampire, you don't even have to be concerned about drowning; Undead Vampires don't breathe (except for talking).

Vampires can't enter a domain unless invited—Wrong.

All Vampires are undead creatures—Wrong: By now, you should understand the difference between Living Vampires and Undead Vampires.

All Vampires are evil demonic creatures—Wrong: Vampires are not demonic creatures. As with walking blood bags, there are good Vampires and there are bad Vampires (by choice).

Vampires have to kill to feed—Wrong: With a little maturity, you will learn that you don't have to take so much blood that you kill while feeding.

Vamps (female Vampires) are tramps—Wrong: While I have seen some Vamps using their womanly ways to entice walking blood bags for food; not all Vamps are like that.

Vampires are repelled by holy objects–Wrong: There may be a few Vampires, especially Undead Vampires, who have a guilt complex and a disdain for holy objects, but crosses and holy water will not keep them away.

All Vampires are Hungarian—Wrong. There are many different Vampires throughout the world. There is hardly a country or culture that doesn't have Vampires. [See CHAPTER 10: VAMPIRES AROUND THE WORLD]

Bram Stoker's Dracula *was a mythical creation of the famous author*—Are you sure?

CHAPTER FIVE
VAMPIRE HISTORY

"If ever there was in the world a warranted and proven history it is that of Vampires."
Jean-Jacques Rousseau (1712-1788)

There is not a lot of Vampire history because Vampires are very reclusive by nature. The fear of attack or being sent into a state of oblivion by Vampire Hunters could be a good explanation for this trait.

In the Beginning ...

I cannot verify the true beginning of Vampires. There are a few "old ones" who might have something to say on the subject of the beginning of Vampirism, but one thing "old ones" have in common—they are super reclusive. Forget about ever talking to one.

I did have the fascinating experience of spending an evening with a real live Vampire historian; that's to say: a historian who is a Vampire. He told me he had come across numerous tales of the first Vampire. The only one he found to be credible through occult writings is as follows:

In the second chapter of the book of Genesis in *The Holy Bible,* God created Adam and said it is not good for man to be alone, so he created Eve. ...

Hold the phone! There are a number of occult studies which claim that Eve was not Adam's first wife. These studies state that Lilith was Adam's first wife. It is said that Lilith was a real bitch, so God removed her from Eden and started over again with Eve. Stories continue that

Figure 2 Lilith

Lilith, expelled from Eden and was the first to eat the meat of animals. She was doing so before God decreed it, so, as a result on her death, Lilith arose as the first Vampire. Later when Eve got Adam and herself thrown out of Eden and the two had children, Lilith found revenge by feeding off the sons and daughters of Adam and Eve. (NOTE: Some occult writings have Lilith as the first witch!)

Greek mythology claims that Zeus and his wife, Hera, accidently created the first Vampire. Zeus had an affair with Poseidon's daughter, Lamia. Their affair begot many children. In a jealous rage, Hera killed all of Lamia's children in Lamia's presence.

Lamia went crazy with grief and started killing any children she could by consuming their blood. Later, she moved on to men. Lamia became the first Vampire and begot a race of Greek Vampires that some Greeks believe kill men and children even today. (Greek mythology has Zeus as the creator of Werewolves ... but that's another story! See *Wolfman Owner's Manual* for more on this.)

Ancient writing pertaining to the existence of Vampires can be found among many cultures. Vampires can be found in early writings among Greek, Roman and Asian cultures, to name a few.

DRACULA 1430-1476

Figure 3 Vlad Tepes, better known as DRACULA. Source: Wikipedia, Public Domain as copyright has expired.

The Vampire historian informed me that historically there was a real living Dracula, so I looked up the information, which is found below. It is true that what follows is about a historical living human, but there is a strong possibility that at his death, he may have become an Undead Vampire. There are events in his life that would seem to verify this. During his life: Dracula: 1) was known as a late practitioner of cannibalism; 2) consumed the blood of his victims; and 3) denounced his Orthodox faith as a condition for release from prison.

In the Alpine mountains by the Arges River are found the ruins of Castle Dracula and the nearby villages, just as Bram Stoker described them in his novel.

Dracula was in fact an authentic 15th century Wallachia prince. He was born in Schaseburg, Transylvania, in 1430. His parents named him Vlad. In 1431, his father was made prince of Wallachia. With the crowning of a new ruler, the family name was changed from Tepes to Dracul (meaning Devil or Dragon). The new prince, a mighty warrior, became one of the guardians of Europe against invasions from the East by Turks and Mongols. The kingdom was set up by Constantinople as a buffer zone to protect the civilized societies against the barbaric societies of the Turks and the Mongols. This included terrorizing the barbaric cultures into fearing aggression from Europe.

The Vampire historian informed me that there was a real living Dracula, so I looked up the information, which is found below. It is true that what follows is about a historical living human, but there is a strong possibility that at his death, he may have become an Undead Vampire. There are events in his life that would seem to verify this.

During his life: Dracula: 1) was known as a late practitioner of cannibalism, 2) consumed the blood of his victims, and 3) denounced his

Orthodox faith as a condition for release from prison.

In the Alpine mountains by the Arges River are found the ruins of Castle Dracula and the nearby villages, just as Bram Stoker described them in his novel.

Dracula was in fact an authentic 15th century Wallachia prince. He was born in Schaseburg, Transylvania in 1430. His parents named him Vlad. In 1431, his father was made prince of Wallachia. With the crowning of a new ruler, the family name was changed from Tepes to Dracul (meaning Devil or Dragon). The new prince, a mighty warrior, became one of the guardians of Europe against invasions from the East by Turks and Mongols. The kingdom was set up by Constantinople as a buffer zone to protect the civilized societies against the barbaric societies of the Turks and the Mongols. This included terrorizing the barbaric cultures into fearing aggression from Europe.

In 1447, Prince Dracul was killed, and his son, the new prince, carried on the fight. On the death of his father, Vlad took his father's throne and responsibilities and had himself crowned Dracula, which literally meant the "son of the Devil".

Dracula was often described in contemporary German, Byzantine, Slovak and Turkish documents as "an awesome, cruel and possibly demented ruler". (McNally& Florescu, *In Search of Dracula*, Connecticut 1972) He was known for his amount of blood spilling and ingenious tortures. Romanian historians labeled him "the Impaler" because of his favorite implement of torture and death.

He also took his father's oath against the Turks. He developed a reputation as a great warrior and a tricky, cunning and brutal man, who was suspicious of everyone. He was also known for his delight in torturing his victims.

In all Central Europe, you can hear peasant folklore about Dracula the Great. Peasants usually praise him because he confined his tortures to the rich and Turkish soldiers. To the peasants, Dracula was a brave warrior known for his military power. He was a hero, saving them from the barbaric Turks. It was reported that in August 1460, Dracula had 30,000 Turks killed in one day.

The ruler was given the name "the Impaler" in ancient writings because of his favorite way of torturing his victims to death. He would have his men put a stake in a victim in such a way that it would not kill the poor wretch instantly. The torture often lasted from many hours to many days. He had various ways of impalement, depending upon age, rank or sex. He often performed these tortures on the outskirts of cities for all to see.

Dracula also delighted in hammering nails through his victim's heads, mutilating their limbs, blinding them, strangling them, burning them alive, cutting off their noses and ears and cutting out sex organs. He scalped his victims, skinned them alive, let them die from exposure to the elements, be torn to bits by wild animals, and burned alive. His victims were hardly ever buried because he enjoyed seeing them rot.

Despite his "interests"' in Transylvania, Wallachia was where he ruled, within his main castle, for three times—first in 1447, again from 1456 to 1462 and finally for two months in 1476. On the northern frontier of Wallachia, facing Transylvania, Dracula built his famous castle. It was his capital and a place full of his horrors. It was there that Dracula was finally killed. Transylvania was the home of his summer castle and is believed to be the castle Bram Stoker used in his work.

In 1462, Dracula was betrayed and was placed in jail where he spent twelve years. The events of these years are easily followed through reading Kurytsin's letters to the Grand Duke of Moscow and through the comments made in some Italian sources. Dracula stayed on good terms with his guards, who kept him supplied with small animals, mice, rats and birds which he tortured by cutting them up or sticking them on small poles, just as he enjoyed doing with his human victims as a free man.

Nicholas of Maryssa, who met Dracula at that time, wrote, "He was not very tall, but very stocky and strong, with a cruel and terrible appearance, a long straight nose, distended nostrils and a thin and reddish face in which the large, wide-open green eyes were framed by bushy black eyebrows, which made them appear threatening."

Dracula married King Mathias's sister and changed his faith from Orthodox to become a Catholic as the King wished and was set free. (Greek Orthodox writings have it that denouncing your faith will prevent your dead body from resting after death, and your undead body will forever roam in a state of unrest—becoming a Vampire?)

In 1474, Dracula's new wife gave birth to a boy, baptized with the name Milbraid, but who was later known as "Milbnea the Bad." In 1476, Dracula, determined to regain his lost lands, met with Bathory and held a war council in Turda. By July 31, Dracula's new army was in central Transylvania. By November, Wallachia was once again under Dracula's control. After his throne was secured, Bathory and his army left. It was too soon, for Dracula was not strong enough to fight off a Turkish invasion. After only two months on the throne, Dracula was killed at the age of forty-five. Historical accounts do not reveal who killed him, but we do know that Dracula was decapitated. His head was sent to the rulers of Constantinople where it was displayed on a pole for the people to see.

Before you start assuming that a Turkish enemy soldier killed Dracula—don't. Some tales have it that Dracula was killed by some of his own men. Stories have it that he would sometimes disguise himself and personally slip over into enemy ranks to assess the enemy strengths or weaknesses for himself. As the story goes, on returning, some soldiers mistook him for an enemy soldier and killed him. One story has it that the soldiers knew it was Dracula in disguise and used the situation to kill their dangerously evil ruler! All stories of Dracula's death have him decapitated, which was performed to keep a dead Vampire from regenerating.

Monks from the Island Monastery of Snogou secretly took Dracula's headless body and placed it in an unmarked grave on their island. There are legions of tales about Dracula's ghost appearing on and around the island. Dracula's wife became a nun at Snogou after her husband's death, possibly to guard her husband's remains or to keep his ghost company.

Rumor has it that Dracula's grave was just in front of the main altar. In 1931, the Romanian Commission on Historic Moments hired George Florescu and Dinu Rosetti to look for Dracula's grave. A grave was found, but it was not Dracula's. However, further digging did bring up a grave the same size as the one found in front of the main altar. This coffin contained no skull, and had some cloth on the bones that could have belonged to Dracula. The material was so fine that it could have only been worn by a ruler. Also found in the grave was some jewelry that was known to be Dracula's, including a bracelet bearing the family crest. According to Rev. G. Dunitria, a neighboring priest, the reason for the move was fear of desecration. Under the disguise of repairs to the church, the move was kept secret. The account given by the priest matched with the known facts about the repairs to the church.

The only existing life-size portrait of Dracula is located in Castle Ambres. Castle Ambres is a huge museum of rogues and monsters. The painting can be found hanging between the wolfman Gonulvas and his two wolf children completely covered with hair (on the right) and Gregor Baxi, a Hungarian who lived a year with a spear through his head. Several portraits of Vlad (Dracula) survived in primitive woodcuts done by Germans.

German Short Stories

Most of these stories are found on German woodcuts which were the main media of the 15th century for matters given to the public. Dracula had Benesti in Wuetzerland burned to the ground, then had the villagers chained and taken to be impaled.

Young princes and nobles from many lands were sent to Wallachia to learn the language and customs. Dracula invited them all to see him, and when they came together, Dracula, fearing they were spies, had the room locked and all four hundred people burned alive. He also had men stripped and shot; he had some roasted and skinned alive. On one occasion, he impaled all six hundred merchants from Wuetzerland to Prezel and took all their goods.

Figure 4 Wood Carving of Vlad the Impaler at work a.k.a. Dracula, Wikipedia, Public Domain as copyright has expired.

Once he had a mistress who announced she was pregnant with his child. Dracula had her cut open under her breasts and had everybody see "where I have been and where my fruits lay."

Sometimes Dracula had children roasted alive and forced their mothers to eat them.

Then the mothers were roasted, and the husbands had to eat the mothers. The men were then impaled.

Once he had a great pot made with two handles and over it a staging device with planks. Through it he had holes made so a man could fall through. Dracula had a huge fire made underneath the pot and poured water in on the victims and boiled them to death. Mothers with children were impaled. Children's heads were impaled on their mother's cut breasts.

Dracula compelled his subjects to practice cannibalism. He was known to drink blood and eat human flesh as well. (Remember: Latent cannibalism and consumption of blood may cause one to rise after death as an Undead Vampire.)

Germans were not the only ones who wrote of Dracula. The Turks did as well. One Russian leader in the 15th century was also interested in Dracula, so Russian ambassadors would write lengthy reports of Dracula's valor and misdeeds. Nicholas of Madrussa reported to the Vatican concerning Dracula and an incident that took place in 1464; it pertained to a specific massacre where Dracula killed 40,000 men and women. The descriptions of Dracula's actions were familiar but horrific nonetheless. Nicholas wrote, "He killed some by breaking them under the wheels of carts; others stripped of their clothes were skinned alive up to their entrails; others were placed upon stakes, or roasted on red-hot coals placed under them; others were punctured with stakes piercing their heads, their breasts, their buttocks and the middle of their entrains with the stake emerging from their mouths; and in order that no form of cruelty be missing, he stuck stakes in both the mother's breasts and thrust their babies unto them. Finally, he killed others in various ferocious ways: torturing them with many kinds of instruments such as the atrocious cruelties of the most frightful tyrant could devise." Vatican archives still hold secret reports sent to Pope Pius the Second.

The Turks wrote of Dracula's campaigns and of the horrible tortures that followed. It seems there was always a stake in the courtyard ready for a Turk.

The Germans wrote of Dracula's sadistic sexual tortures. When Dracula's first wife (the first of three wives) was proved to be unfaithful, Dracula cut out her sexual organs, skinned her alive and exposed her in public with her skin hanging on poles. Similar tortures were applied to unfaithful unmarried maidens who gave up their virginity and to those who were proven not chaste. In other times, Dracula would have the nipples of women's breasts removed or cause a fiery hot iron to be slowly inserted into the victim's vagina until the rounded end of the point entered their mouths.

To this day, it's said that the ghost of Dracula can be seen roaming "Dracula country"!

ERZSEBET (ELIZABETH) BATHORY 1560-1614

**Figure 5 ERZSEBET (ELIZABETH) BATHORY Wikipedia, Public
Domain as copyright has expired.**

Some believe Elizabeth Báthory, "The Blood Countess", was not just a famous serial killer, but may very well have been a Living Vampire! She was a Living Vampire impervious to laws or morays by nature of her blue blood and family lineage. She felt free to be as extravagant as she wished in her bloody pursuits.

Also known as "The Blood Countess of Transylvania," it is interesting to note that she was a distant relative of Dracula. It was the Bathorys who helped Dracula regain his throne one last time.

As to her family, the noble Báthory family stemmed from the Hun Gutkeled clan which held power in broad areas of East Central Europe (in those places now known as Poland, Hungary, Slovakia and Romania) and emerged to assume a role of relative eminence by the first half of the 13th century. Abandoning their tribal roots, they assumed the name of one of their estates (Bátor meaning "valiant") as a family name. Their power rose in the mid-16th century to include great kings, princes, members of the judiciary, as well as holders of ecclesiastical and civil posts.

It is said that Elizabeth grew up to be a beautiful, tall, shapely young lady who was immensely proud of her light creamy complexion. Married to an aristocratic soldier at age fifteen, she became the Countess of the Castle of Csijthe. It was a lonely existence with her castle deep within the Carpathian Mountains of Transylvania and her husband away for long stretches of time, at war with the Turks.

During Elizabeth's twenty-fifth year, her uncle Stephan, a prince of Transylvania, became Stephen Bathory, King of Poland. When she was in her forties, her husband was killed fighting the Turks. With the death of her husband, Elizabeth started considering a new husband, but was upset at her less than perfect complexion that had come with age and birthing six children. Story has it that one night a servant accidently pulled the Countess's hair while combing it out. The Countess, upset with her completion in the mirror, struck out at her servant with such ferocity that she drew blood. Later the Countess discovered that her skin where the servant had bled on her looked younger. With verification by visiting scholars of the healing power of virgin blood, The Blood Countess was born!

For her blood treatments to work, the Blood Countess needed lots of virgin blood …

TALES OF THE BLOOD COUNTESS

Tales have it that she had a number of witches or Vampires hired to roam the countryside, looking for young viral female virgins to continue her nightly bloody beauty treatments. She would promise jobs at the castle to young peasant women, then force them to the dungeons where her assistants would hang them upside down and slit their throats. The fresh blood captured in bowls would be immediately poured into the Blood Countess' bath while the blood was still warm.

Tales also say that she went from hanging the women to drain them of blood for her nightly bloodbaths to inventing torture devices specialized in draining blood directly into her bloody bath tub.

This tale (and my personal favorite) said the Blood Countess had a customized iron maiden, designed to look like a beautiful naked female. It was designed so that a virgin victim would be forced to hug her special creation, then spikes would project from the monster creation's neck, breasts and mound of Venus, right into the screaming victim's corresponding body parts. Then the assistants of the Blood Countess would squeeze the two fatal lovers together, pressing out as much blood as possible.

While the above sounds so lusciously pleasing to me, a Vampire, I tend to believe the alternate tale that she designed a female-shaped iron maiden that better suited the shape of her victims. An iron maiden traditionally was an iron-shaped upright coffin with spikes inside the coffin door. As the torturer slowly squeezed the coffin shut, the multiple spikes would penetrate the victim and cause their death. The Blood Countess had her shapely instrument of death designed with holes in the back of the feet so the virgin blood flowed right into her bloody beautification bathtub!

It is said that when she failed to get the desired results, she started drinking the blood she was bathing in and later even took to consuming the flesh of her victims. Eventually sixty to six hundred dead and drained female bodies were found in and around her Bloody Castle of Death, still waiting to be buried. Remember: the taking of blood and latent cannibalism are two ways a walking blood bag may become an Undead Vampire at death!

Note that history records all the Blood Countess's assistants were executed in the style one would execute Vampires: heads decapitated and bodies burned! The ashes were then spread out in multiple areas, in non-sanctified grounds like graveyards or church grounds.

The fact that the court ordered the walling up of The Blood Countess would indicate that they feared they were jailing a Living Vampire, and the lack of an opening larger than for insertion of food would signify a fear of her possessing or at some point gaining the ability to use Vampire enthrallment on her guards. (Enthrallment: A form of controlling through hypnotism.) Surely they weren't afraid that her beauty alone could sway a jailer to let her escape her home imprisonment. Sounds like the making of an Undead Vampire to me, if she wasn't already a Living Vampire.

BRAM STOKER 1847-1912

Figure 6 Bram Stoker; Wikipedia, Public Domain as copyright has expired.

Bram Stoker is not and was never a Vampire! So why is he part of Vampire history? Have you ever known anyone to affect Vampire history like this man? He wasn't even the first to write about Vampires. After he wrote *Dracula,* Vampire existence has never been the same.

In 1897, Bram Stoker published his novel entitled *Dracula.* It was an overnight bestseller. In 1899, the novel was published in America, and again it became a bestseller. It is still popular; I have heard multiple times that the only book more popular and more printed than *Dracula* is *The Holy Bible.*

On May 17, 1897, just a few days before Bram Stoker's *Dracula* was published, the character, Count Dracula, appeared in a play titled *Dracula or the Undead.* The play, strictly based on the book, was four hours long. Starring in it was an unknown Hungarian actor named Bela Lugosi.

Stoker invented some myths about Vampires in his novel, as well as using some already written, such as his thoughts on how a Vampire looks. "His face was strong—a very strong aquiline, with a high bridge of the thin nose and peculiarly arched nostrils, with a lofty domed forehead, and hair growing scantily round the temples but profusely elsewhere. His eyebrows were very massive, almost meeting over the nose, and with bush hair that seemed to curl in its own profusion. The mouth, so far as I could see it under the heavy mustache, was fixed and rather civil-looking, with peculiarly sharp white teeth; these protruded over the lips, whose remarkable ruddiness bowed astonishing vitality in a man of his years. For the rest, his ears were pale, and at the tops extremely pointed; the chin was broad and strong, and the cheeks firm." Later in the story, through the character Harker, we see Dracula in his grave, and the description is a great deal like the peasants gave researchers in the seventies. He also notices how Dracula looks younger after "blood feedings," hence Dracula's immortality.

In a confrontation between Dracula and Harker, Stoker reveals his knowledge of the real Dracula (Vlad Tepes).

Through the Van Helsing character, Stoker tells us of vampirism (some of which he invented himself): "…Take it, then, that the Vampire, and the belief of his limitations and his cure, rest for the moment on the same base. For, let me tell you, he is known everywhere that men have been. In old Greece, in old Rome, he flourished in Germany all over, in France, in India, even in the Chersonese and in China, so far from us in all ways, they're over here. …The Vampire lives on, and cannot die by mere passing of the time. He can flourish when that he can fatten on the blood of the living. Even more, we have seen amongst us that he can even grow younger; that his vital faculties strenuous. … He throws no shadow; he makes in the mirror no reflection. He can transform himself to wolf, as we gather from the ship arrival in Whitby: …he can be as bat …he can come in mist which he creates. …Then there are things, which so afflict him that he has no power, as the garlic that we know of and as for things sacred, as this symbol, my crucifix …There are others, too, which I shall tell you of, lest in our seeking we may need them. The branch of wild rose on his coffin keep him that he move not from it; a sacred bullet fired into the coffin kills him so he be true dead; and as for a stake through him, we know already of its peace; or the cut-off head that giveth rest."

Dracula meets his death just at sundown when Van Helsing slices off the Vampire's head, and Dr. Steward plunges a stake into his heart. Dracula immediately turns to dust.

You'd think that would finish Dracula. But does it? Later in the movies, we begin to understand that traditional methods of killing do not work completely on Vampires like Dracula.

CHAPTER SIX
VAMPIRE FRIENDS AND FIENDS

Dhampir
    Definition: Vampire half-breed; See Vampyr

Djadadjii
    Definition: This is a specific kind of Vampire Hunter from Bulgaria. He puts out a large jar with blood in it to entice a Vampire to enter the jar. Once the Vampire enters, the Djadadjii corks the jar, which traps the Vampire. The jar is then tossed into a large fire to destroy the being.

Ghoul
    Definitions: 1) An evil spirit or demon that plunders graves and feeds on the dead; 2) grave robber; and 3) one who delights in the revolting, morbid or loathsome. (Some say I fit that description. What do you think?)
    If you want a quick, painful death, just call a Vampire a ghoul! WE ARE NOT GHOULS! Call a Vampire a ghoul, and he or she will go through you like a multi-blade chainsaw, tossing your bloody body parts in so many directions that no one will ever find all of you again. I can't emphasize this enough—Vampires and Undead Vampires are not ghouls!
    One reason we are so tender about this is that, not often, but sometimes, a blood bag will become a ghoul while being turned instead of becoming a Vampire. It is not known why this happens, and fortunately, this hardly ever happens. When it does, I can't imagine a

Vampire allowing the failure to continue to exist.

Mulo

Definition: Gypsy term for "One who is dead."

As gypsies know no borders, Mulos can differ depending on the area. Basically, a Mulo is a common European Vampire.

Nosferatu

Definition: Greek term for "plague-carrier."

This species of Vampire is said to be the illegitimate child of parents who were illegitimate. Soon after its burial, the Nosferatu embarks on a long career of destruction. It delights in tormenting and engaging in wild orgies with the living. The male can father children. The Nosferatu hates newly married couples due to its own illegitimacy and wreaks its revenge on such couples by making the groom impotent and the bride barren.

Vampiridzhija

Definition: A vampiridzhija is a professional Bulgarian Vampire Hunter.

Vampire Hunter

Definition: 1) one who hunts Vampires to end their existence; 2) one on a holy quest to rid the world of Vampires; and 3) demon hunter.

Unfortunately, there are those who are prejudiced against Vampires and feel it's their holy duty to wipe out all demonic, evil Vampires (meaning all Vampires).

I have been lucky enough not to have had a run-in with a Vampire Hunter personally. There is some concern that a Vampire Hunter may try to hunt me down through my publisher, but certain precautions have been set up to prevent this.

I interviewed a Vampire who loved telling the tale of how he got a Vampire Hunter off his case …

"I'm not an evil Vampire. I have never killed to feed. I'll either purchase my blood at my local grocery store or (for the fun of it) go to a Vampire club not far from my domain.

I was in my local bank (monetary, not blood bank!) withdrawing funds from my account, when a man waving a shotgun fired off a round and ordered everyone to hit the floor. I didn't feel like missing my appointment, so I approached the evildoer with the idea of removing the offensive weapon by enthralling him using a form of Vampire hypnosis. Unfortunately, before I succeeded, he fired the offensive weapon point blank into me. I lost my temper, as he had just ruined my favorite suit— you know how difficult it is to get fine French silk shirts in America! I took the offending weapon away from him with such force some of his fingers came with it. I couldn't handle his incessant screaming, so I ripped off his head. The populace in the bank started screaming. Instead of ripping off all their heads, I ran out of the bank, so fast that they didn't see me leave.

Later, on the news, the foolish populace of the bank claimed I just vanished into thin air, like magic—fools. From the news, you would have thought I was the fiend, not the would-be bank robber. It didn't seem to occur to any one that I had just stopped a bank robber in the act, and most likely prevented a multiple killing. The robber sure showed his willingness to kill, as seen by his quick trigger finger, which was used on me."

"Wouldn't you know a Vampire Hunter, posing as a police detective, successfully got information on me at the bank? He used the information to track me down at my domicile: He literally broke into my home! He must have assumed I would be sleeping the (dead) sleep of the Undead Vampire. I'm not undead, and my home defenses woke me and allowed me to get the drop on him. As he crept into my darkened room, I simply pounced on him from behind the door. It could not have been easier!

I have never killed to eat, and I wasn't going to start with this Vampire-hunting fool. Wondering what to do with this Vampire Hunter, I got this crazy idea. I went right for his throat to feed on him. He was so sure he was about to die that he was a delightful meal, so full of his fear of dying!

Instead of feeding to his death, I cut my wrist right in front of his wide fear-filled eyes and ordered him to drink. For fear of his life, he did feed and I turned him!

After he recovered, you can imagine the fun I was about to have! I gleefully informed him he was now one of the hunted. Then I threw him out.

"I have no idea what happened to him after that." Smiling he added, "Maybe he went to one of his Vampire-hunting friends, and they took less than pity on him and killed him, as one of the demonic dammed."

"I have not been bothered by any other hunters since."

"There was this big bad motorcycle loner and Vampire Hunter…" a Living Vampire biker started telling me one night while clubbing. "I began showing off during a bar brawl, tossing rival bikers around like they were rag dolls. After the fun of the fighting, and the destruction of the place, I went across the street to my motel room. I had a young mama (a female motorcycle groupie, usually kept around to be sexually tossed around the motorcycle gang.) over my shoulder. She wasn't complaining from the caveman treatment. Back in my motel room, I planted her in one of the beds and started revving her engines … if you know what I mean. The goal was to get her properly seasoned for my dinner. She was very ready for me to put the bite on her when the door crashed open and this biker Vampire Hunter smashes in, diving at me with a stake in his hand. The stake hurt like hell! He missed my heart and plunged the stake into my stomach. His landing on top of the mama to get to me had her screaming up a storm right into my ear—I clubbed her upside the head to shut her up."

He continued his tale, "Caught off guard, I was slow to respond to the intrusion of the Vampire Hunter, but seeing my dinner ruined with the mama out cold, I pulled the stake out of my stomach and almost plunged it into the Vampire Hunter. As my stomach started to heal, I observed the total terror on the face of the Vampire Hunter, and realized I still had dinner coming."

"Giving my stomach a little more time to recover, I spoke, 'In the future you'd better make sure you hit the heart … assuming you have a next time.'"

"I had no intention of killing him; I was just spicing him up some.

To that end I added, 'I had no plans on killing this sweet little mama ...'

"Adding venom to my voice, I continued, 'but you are another story.' "Seeing the effect of my words properly seasoning him, I had a very nice dinner from the Vampire Hunter. During my dining, he passed out. Noticing a wedding ring on the Vampire Hunter, I had a little fun positioning the Vampire Hunter and the half-naked little mama in an uncompromising position. Enjoying my jest, I walked through the smashed doorway. Outside I took a moment to enjoy the night air, then jumped on my bike and roared off."

Vamps

Definition: Female Vampires.

Even though this is a proper term for a female Vampire, be careful using it around them. Some Vamps act as if you called them "tramps." This might have come about because of horror movies depicting female Vampires as sexual tramps.

While I'm not saying all Vamps are tramps, I have seen quite a number of female Vampires dressing and/or acting like tramps in Vampire Bars and Clubs, with the purpose of enticing their next meal.

Beware using the term around female Vampires. While Vampires heal quickly, after calling her a "vamp," I thought the nail scratches that a female Vampire gave my face in a rage would never heal.

Vampyr (Vampeer)

Definition: a Vampire half-breed; one sired by a Vampire father and a blood bag (human) mother (already pregnant).

How does a sterile Vampire sire a baby? He puts the bite on an already pregnant blood bag. The result is a Vampyr. Personally, I can't see why a Vampire would want to feed on a pregnant mother. Male Vampires are not the family type; it's that lone wolf thing.

In my travels and research, I have never seen or heard of a real Vampyr. But I have been told they can and do exist.

I'm told a Vampyr is just like a Living Vampire, but they age at a much slower rate than blood bags once they reach blood bag maturity.

Since Vampyrs age, they also die like blood bags. This raises the question: Does a Vampyr rise as a full Undead Vampire at death? No one has ever been able to answer that question for me.

Supposedly, Vampyr have all the heightened advantages of a Living Vampire without the need to feed on blood, or much less need to feed. I have not been able to verify anything about Vampyr, as I have never seen a real Vampyr.

There are a number of Vampyr in the various forms of media, like Blade, Vampire Hunter D (Sons of Dracula?) and/or Ariel from Darkchylde fame. It's interesting that they all seem to become Vampire Hunters!

Werewolf

Definition:1) a human who becomes a wolf-man during the phase of the full moon; 2) one who experiences lycanthropy changes during the cycle of the new moon; 3) shape-shifter. For more on this Read Wolfman Owner's Manual.

Come now, you're not going to tell me you are surprised to hear there are werewolves. All this time you have been reading about Vampires and you're surprised to hear that there are werewolves.

Unfortunately, there are plenty of werewolves. Vampires hate werewolves and werewolves hate Vampires … violently!

For one thing, Vampires can smell a werewolf from blocks away, even while they are in blood bag form. Werewolves smell even worse than wet dogs. Most Vampires can't even be in the same room with a werewolf (in any form) without upchucking blood! (Blood is the life … we hate upchucking blood.)

Unfortunately, werewolves can also smell out Vampires (living or undead) while in human or werewolf form.

I have heard of Vampire Hunters who are werewolves. Werewolves in their wolf form have been known to hunt down and kill Vampires just to kill Vampires!

One reason we hate werewolves is that most werewolves act as if they are cursed: *Poor little me. I turn into an amazing creature of the night during the full moon.* Right, like they don't enjoy the freedom of running wild or the pure pleasure of the hunt in wolf form.

Considering a Vampire can't get near a werewolf because of their smell, I can't imagine what werewolf blood must taste like—UGH, just the thought turns my stomach!

Fortunately, in my travels, I have never confronted a werewolf, but more than a couple of times on arriving within a new town, I have smelled a werewolf from a distance. When this happens, I just keep on keeping on.

CHAPTER SEVEN
VAMPIRE ECONOMICS

A Vampire can live very cheaply. Find a hole to hide your coffin and steal your food right from the necks of blood bags—if you call that living or unliving.

If your choice is to live much as you did as a walking blood bag and continue living in a residence, be it apartment or private estate, you'll at least have fewer bills to pay…

Your food bill will be greatly reduced, since you only live on and purchase blood at the grocery store.

As environmental temperature is not a concern to Vampires who are not affected by temperature changes, your utility bills will be less. You might want to remember to turn on the heat or air conditioner when or if you are having visitors.

You will have a smaller utility bill from little need for lights. With your enhanced night sight, you'll be happier with the lights off.

If you use a car to get around, you might as well keep it. Remember, unlike in the movies, you don't change into a bat and fly. If you are undead, you can save on transportation cost by mist flying. Also, remember you can run *extremely* fast for quite some distance, without being seen.

You are going to have a nice long life (or unlife), so live it in style. Eventually, you're going to want to change your lifestyle and your identity so that all those getting older around you don't take notice that you're not getting older with them. There are Vampires who specialize in falsifying documentation to produce a whole new identity for you. For instance, let's say that new life includes the new name Ted Mitchell. Put out a large insurance policy on yourself and make or change a will so that everything goes to Ted Mitchell. Leave your total estate to the new you a few times over many years and you'll be a multi-millionaire in no time.

Another option is to live the life of a road bum and just keep travelling like I do, the life of a gambler. This has suited me fine for years. I fully enjoy the free life of a roaming gambler, I just make a point of not winning to the point of making a spectacle of myself and after a while, I move on. By the time I start repeating places I have been to before, too many years have passed for anyone to remember me—for the most part.

I was at this gambling house out west once where an old geezer recognized me as the son of a great gambler that had passed through many years before. He gave me an earful about how my father had cleaned him out so completely that his wife-to-be walked out on him for losing their wedding and honeymoon money.

I just made a point of leaving sooner, before the old guy put two and two together and came up with the right answers. This has only happened once, and I figure if I just don't visit the place again for another twenty years, I'll be fine.

That reminds me of the time I visited the grave of an old soldier at the famous Arlington Cemetery on a whim. I was visiting a soldier's grave that was really mine. The coffin actually had some soldier whose identity I stole. When I left, I was stopped and spoke to an old guy who thought he recognized me. When he saw how young I appeared, he assumed I must have been this soldier buddy's son. He even went so far as to suggest that I should visit him so he could tell me tales of my heroic dead father. I promised I would and then disappeared.

It makes sense. You live a very long time and you are going to accrue a large amount of money. Just keep building up your funds and rolling it over to your new identity and keep getting richer.

Personally, I find too much money a problem. I spend some evenings just losing at the gambling table to unload excess cash. I can only carry so much. You don't want to give it away in big tips and get noticed. Who takes notice of a gambler having a bad night at the table?

Possible Careers for a Vampire

Assassin (Living Vampire)

You're a supernatural predator. What target, natural or supernatural, has a chance against you while you are on the hunt? You could hit a target with a sniper rifle and not even need a scope. Take the more hands-on approach (not to mention fangs), and the more guards the target has, the more of a smorgasbord you have while just doing your job.

While possible, this career would be more difficult for an Undead Vampire; it requires a lot of travel and you may not want to be hampered by working only at night.

Gambler (Living Vampire)

This is my personal favorite, for it has served me well over my lifetime as a Vampire. Being constantly on the road, you don't have to be bothered changing identities to protect your immortality. You do have to have a love for the cards and some abilities with the games.

Unless you plan on being a house gambler and play only one location, this may not be a good career for an Undead Vampire because of the traveling. By law, you can't own a gambling house and gamble at that establishment. Gambling at one location over years does create the problem of being seen not to age.

Graveyard watchman (Living or Undead Vampire)

This career has the advantage of coming with its own private dwelling … and all the meals you can dig up! Just joking; a little of my ghoulish humor coming out to play.

With your heightened sense and abilities, no natural or supernatural being is going to get anywhere near the sleeping dead that you are guarding without you knowing it! If someone or something is stupid enough to try, you have yourself a meal in the line of duty! (That's assuming your intruder is a grave robber and not a ghoul.) Please don't tell me you are surprised to hear there are ghouls in the night. Have I not mentioned the disturbing fact that for some unknown reason a "turning" sometimes goes wrong and produces a ghoul instead of an honorable Vampire?

Night Watchman (Living or Undead Vampire)

Again, with your supernatural abilities, no natural or supernatural being is going to get anywhere near who or what you are guarding without you knowing it. If someone or something is stupid enough to try, you have yourself a meal in the line of duty.

Personal Security Guard (Living or Undead Vampire)

Walking blood bags pay very well for their personal security, especially if they have a reason. Your abilities will make it very difficult for enemies to get anywhere near your charge while you are on guard without you knowing it! If someone or something is stupid enough to try you have yourself a meal in the line of duty.

Police officer (Living or Undead Vampire)

Your Vampiric abilities could take you far in the career of law enforcement. Once trained and out on the street, you will have to be careful not to give yourself away using your natural advanced abilities in the line of duty. Vampire Hunters don't care if you are one of the good guys; to a Vampire Hunter there is no such thing as a good Vampire!

If you are careful, you could easily advance in the career of law enforcement; as long as you have the aptitude for the job.

This may be an impossible career for an Undead Vampire: I don't believe police provide night only police academies. If as a blood bag or as a Living Vampire you have had police training, you could have fake paperwork specially designed to have you transferring in for night duty.

Soldier (Living Vampire):

With proper training, your superior combatant abilities will make you a real asset on any battlefield. Feeding off the dying after a battle may be more difficult than in the older less mechanized war days.

Shepherd (Living or Undead Vampire):

Guarding livestock would be a nice job especially for an Undead Vampire. While guarding the livestock, you could feed off them by just taking a little from a number of critters each night. If done carefully: who'd be the wiser? Your abilities will make it very difficult for enemies to get anywhere near your charge while you are on guard without you knowing it! If someone or something is stupid enough to try you have yourself a meal in the line of duty!

Traveling salesman (Living Vampire):

I may be showing my age with this suggestion; are there still traveling salesmen? This would not be a career choice for an Undead Vampire because of the traveling requirements of the job. I would not be surprised to find that some of the richest men in the world are secretly *Vampires!*

CHAPTER EIGHT
TO KILL A VAMPIRE

Now it may seem strange to have this material in a Vampire Owner's Manual, but ignorance can kill! How will you know how to spot a Vampire Hunter if you don't know what to look for!

Vampire Hunters

Keep a wary eye on strangers dressed in black with the eyes of a hunter. (A hunter's eyes will be constantly moving, constantly on the search; taking in everything and nothing in particular.) Look for someone wearing a trench coat or duster big enough to hide stakes and a hammer. Some Vampire Hunters may still carry their tools of death in black bags.

A good Vampire Hunter will not confront you openly, but will stalk you to your place of rest and perform his/her deadly deed while you sleep. So always be very careful that you are not tailed back to your coffin or place of rest. I strongly suggest that you take strong consideration as to the accessibility of your coffin or place of rest by a Vampire Hunter.

If the Vampire is undead, killing the Vampire is all the easier. Just move the coffin into sunlight, open it up to the light, then watch the Vampire go up like a lit Lucifer! This is why it's very important for Undead Vampires to give careful consideration as to where to hide their coffin. Remember your ability to turn to mist. Bury your coffin, leaving a very small opening for entering and exiting your coffin in mist form. Just don't make the common mistake of leaving your coffin safely buried in the graveyard. That's the first place any good Vampire Hunter is going to look! All a Vampire Hunter has to do is show up with a horse and walk that horse over all the graves. Horses have a very keen sense for predators and will not walk over a gravesite in which a Vampire is buried. If the horse fails to walk over a grave, the Vampire Hunter digs up the coffin and opens it up to the sunlight, while quickly stepping back as the Vampire lights up like a lit Lucifer!

Killing a Living Vampire is a little more difficult due to their amazing regenerative powers. The traditional way is to pound a stake into the heart of the sleeping Vampire; then remove the head. If the Vampire Hunter really knows his stuff, he will then move the head to another place for separate burial or cremation. If you're lucky, and he only puts a stake in your heart, and if the stake is removed, the heart will regenerate and you are back among the living (or unliving).

If the Vampire Hunter should stake you, decapitate you, and then leave the head in place or nearby, someone could place your head in the right place and remove the stake. Your heart will regenerate; followed by the regeneration of your neck and head, and you're back among the living again!

Bullets

Just a note on bullets: If you are shot by a low caliber bullet, you might not even notice it. A larger bullet might hurt, but it will not kill you because of your amazing regenerative powers. If some psycho militant comes at you with a bazooka or flamethrower—well, that's a different story!

I can speak from experience. I have fought in multiple wars from the Civil War, to World War I and II, the Korean War. (Korean *War*? Wasn't that a police action?), and the Vietnam War. I have been shot with everything from musket balls to the latest in firepower. I have been torn up very badly by grenades, land mines, and I even got torn up real good once by a Bouncing Betty. If you don't know what a Bouncing Betty is … don't ask! I still shiver just thinking about it. (You just had to ask! See Bouncing Betty in the Glossary.) The point is, while I have some painful memories, I'm still here and still in one piece.

Note: Silver bullets are for killing werewolves, not Vampires! A well placed silver bullet in the heart will immobilize a Vampire, if the bullet stays in the heart. But if the bullet is removed or the shot goes through the heart without stopping the Vampire will regenerate.

Boredom

I have heard many times that the major cause of death among Vampires (especially Undead Vampires) is boredom.

After hundreds of years of getting up, hunting for food, and rushing back to your coffin or place of rest before the sun rises—night, after night, after night, the same old thing. Some Vampires just become weary of the same mundane existence and decide to see what a sunrise looks like.

I strongly suggest that you find some hobby or favorite pastime to keep you occupied.

Take me as an example. I spent my time researching this book and gambling, not to mention skirt chasing. The latter two I enjoy immensely and researching this book has not only been personally educational for my lifestyle, but has given me a feeling of accomplishment. I'm not just living it up with my skirt chasing and gambling, but I am being productive with my research and writing.

Once I interviewed a Vampire historian. He loved his work so much that when he discovered there really were Vampires, he hunted one down and begged the Vampire to turn him into a Vampire. Now he continues his favorite pursuit of observing history in the making and writing books on historic subjects. You may have read some of his books under his many different names and did not realize it.

Burning at the stake

This form of execution is most likely a carryover from the Salem Witch Trials. If you're a Living Vampire, this is the worst way to be killed. Every one of your thousands of nerve endings will scream in pain. If you find yourself in this situation, I suggest you really piss off your tormentors. Entice them into creating a *big* bonfire. If the fire around you has a wide enough area, the fire will force the air away from you and you will die from lack of air instead of dying in nerve-screaming pain, I have read that losing your life due to lack of air is like falling asleep, then you

73

die, peacefully and painlessly! Of course, you will only die to revive from a Living Vampire to revive as an Undead Vampire (who does not need air). So keep faking your death, and hope your tormentors will assume you are dead and put the fire out before the fire permanently puts you out!

If your tormentors continue roasting you as an Undead Vampire and the flames get to you, you'll go up like a struck Lucifer and will hardly have time to feel any pain!

This was a very popular way of publically executing convicted Vampires during the 17th and 18th centuries.

Drowning

Basically, you can't drown a Vampire to cause its death. Living Vampires breathe; Undead Vampires don't breathe (except for communication (talking)).

If you drown a Living Vampire and succeed in killing him, you will only produce an Undead Vampire. Undead Vampires don't need to breathe, so you can't drown an Undead Vampire …

I was told of a Living Vampire who was unknowingly being tracked by a Vampire Hunter. She admitted she liked enticing rich men. She would get what she could from them economically, and then make a complete meal blood feasting to the point of death of them. While on a cruise with her latest sugar daddy a Vampire Hunter who gives a young person expensive gifts in return for friendship or intimacy. Unknown, a Vampire Hunter was tracking her onto the cruise ship and was watching her, waiting for the moment to get her alone … waiting for the moment to destroy one more evil Vampire.

"My feed lover (loving blood bag) and I had an argument one night, so I left him for some fresh air and to enjoy the sight of the moon over the ocean. In my mood, I failed to notice I was not alone. Suddenly, I was shoved from behind and found myself going over the side of the cruise ship. I quickly turned, in hopes of grabbing onto the ship's railings, but even at Vampire speed, I wasn't fast enough to prevent my descent from the safety of the ship … into the dark, deep ocean below. One thing I did succeed in doing was to get a good look at the Vampire Hunter who had shoved me over the side of the ship. When I hit the water, I figured I was dead; I mean really dead! Can you imagine my astonishment when I regained conciseness deep under the sea?! First, I started to panic, *"How am I going to breathe? I've got to get up where I can breathe."* Then it just as suddenly occurred to me; I was doing fine and not breathing.

I swam to the surface, not necessarily for air as much as to get my bearings—OK, not breathing under the deep dark sea was a little creepy. Fortunately, I was thrown overboard at night and it was still night when I reached the surface. It hadn't occurred to me yet that I had gone through a change from Living Vampire to Undead Vampire. I discovered the ship was gone, but an island was in sight, so I started swimming for it. Eventually I got so tired I sunk back to the bottom of the sea and rested. While sinking, I had enough sense to keep track of my direction toward the island and after a very quiet tranquil rest under the deep dark sea, I just started walking in the right direction. Bottom walking was less tiring than trying to stay topside, and it really was very tranquil deep under the ocean. Just me and the fishes seemed to give me a sense of space. Despite the darkness, I was able to see well enough with my enhanced night sight. I was off the coast of one of the Bermuda islands, so the water started getting brighter (even deep as I was) as the sun started coming up. I was admiring the view, when I started getting uncomfortably hot under the water.

It was only then that it occurred to me that I was now undead and the rising sun was going to burn me alive (sort of) even under the sea! With the realization that I was now undead, the water around me really started to boil from my anger. Then it sunk in, undead … sunlight, not a good combination. I was starting to boil from the sunlight reaching down to me even deep under the sea. With the increased light upon the area, I discovered a sunken boat nearby and headed for it as quickly as the water pulling against me would allow. As you can tell, I made it to the boat in time and slept the daylight hours away in the lower part of the sunken vessel. "

She continued, "After a good day's sleep. I awoke and continued my voyage toward land. I had made a mental note of the direction of the boat to the island and used that to help keep my direction true, only now I was deeply grinding my fangs in anger. It finally sunk in that I was undead. I had enjoyed day life and the heat of the sun. Hell, I did some of my best fishing for my next rich blood bag lying on the beach, nearly or totally naked, while supposedly sunbathing. I was going to miss sunny days and sunny beaches immensely…when I find that Vampire Hunter, *he was going to miss his head*!"

After visibly getting herself under control, she continued her tale, "To make a long story short …"

(*Too late*)

"…I made it to the island by nightfall and discovered the cruise ship sitting offshore. I made a point of staying away from the cruise ship. I couldn't see myself in any reflection, but figured I was quite a sight after days under the sea *and being undead!*"

"Cruising the island by night, I found my Vampire Hunter, already stalking another (island) Vampire!

I trailed him for a while, deliberately letting him catch a glimpse of me before I'd slip away into a shadow. At first, he passed it off and gave it little thought, but eventually he could not ignore the fact that someone or something was stalking him, and I could feel his fear growing. I stepped out of a shadow and scared him into reaching for a stake … and dropping it, I knew he was ready for …

As I stepped toward him, he eventually lost it so bad that he trapped himself in a closed off alleyway. *This is going to be fun!* At first, he could only see me as a menacing form. He never really saw me until I approached him, deliberately walking under a window of a lit but unused room. You should have seen his eyes enlarge in his enlightenment and so enticing to see his growing fear. He started babbling, "It can't be! …You're not here; you're at the bottom of the sea!"

"You would know…you put me there!" I answered, enjoying the growing fear reforming his face!"

Grinning with the memory of the moment, she continued, "He was so common, would you believe, he fumbled as he pulled out another stake from the tool pouch he was carrying at his side. He then lunged for me …"

"I just simply grabbed his wrist with the stake in it, and grabbed his neck with my other hand, and crushed the wrist holding the would-be weapon of so many Vampire deaths. I so enjoyed the look of desperation overtaking the fear in his face—savored the moment by moving closer and giving him a cold, deadly kiss. I then moved my cold, dead, lips voluptuously to his neck, slowly savoring every moment as I put the bite on him and drank him dry."

After a pause, she continued, "Oh yeah, I then ripped of his head and tossed it a mile into the sea for the fish to feed on."

I just had to ask, "So how did you get off the island in your undead form?"

"My current love knew I was a Vampire, and when I found him away from the cruise ship and told him what had happened to me, he was very understanding. He arranged for us to leave the island by hiring an island jumper to make a night flight."

"And what happened to this thoughtful lover of yours?" I asked.

"He eventually bored me, bugging me to keep him from death's door by making him a Vampire … so I made a complete meal of him and moved on"

I heard of an ancient tale where the villagers held a witch trial. The accused was tied to a chair on the end of a long pole and placed under water. If after the passing of some minutes, the accused came up alive … she was a witch and would be put to the stake to be burned alive. If she drowned to death … it proved she wasn't a witch and her family was permitted to bury her.

What they didn't know was the woman was a Living Vampire and in drowning her, they changed her into an Undead Vampire. She faked her death, and her family was permitted to have her buried, as the authorities had failed to prove her to be a witch.

After her burial, she arose and as an Undead Vampire systematically killed those who had accused her of being a witch.

I am told the village historically no longer exists.

Holy Water

Drink up! Holy water is just blessed water and can't hurt you one bit as you are not a demonic creature from hell.

Stake to the Heart

This is the favorite of Vampire Hunters. A stake to the heart will kill a Living Vampire, but if the Vampire body is not properly prepared by the removal of the head, or if the stake is later removed, a Living Vampire will regenerate as an Undead Vampire. Likewise, an Undead Vampire will regenerate as an Undead Vampire under the right circumstances.

In our modern society, I have heard of a service provided by some Vampire Clubs that give out GPS watches to their Vampire patrons. If as a regular you fail to appear at the club after a certain time, they activate your GPS and go looking for you. If you are found staked, but intact or staked with your parts in sight, they will remove your stake so you can regenerate.

I have not heard if this service has been advantageous for any Vampires.

Sunlight

It's very important for Undead Vampires to remember that sunlight will light them up faster than you can say "PUFF!"

It's wise to keep this in mind when you are finding a place for your (Undead Vampire) coffin. Bury or hide your coffin where a Vampire Hunter can't easily move it into the sunlight while you sleep.

Just a quick note: Death by sunlight is a very popular method of Vampire suicide.

Werewolves vs. Vampires

REMEMBER: If you smell a werewolf in the area, clear out. If you can smell the werewolf, then he can smell you, and if it's that time of the month, he will most likely come after you with the intending to mutilate to death.

Because of your regenerative powers, it is not easy for a werewolf to kill a Vampire, but it can be done. Even if the werewolf fails to kill, he can still inflict lots of pain.

I have heard of some Vampires who carry a small weapon on them loaded with silver bullets just in case of a sudden werewolf attack. I myself used to have a few silver bullets on hand back when I wore a holster rig. In fact, when I learned of the dangers of werewolves, I changed to a double holster rig. I kept one pistol loaded with silver bullets. Werewolves are extremely fast and apparently, can smell a Vampire before a Vampire can smell a werewolf, so it is possible for a werewolf to surprise a Vampire with their superior heightened animalistic sense of smell.

Personally, I have had limited confrontation with werewolves. I have in my travels got a whiff of a werewolf on arriving in a new town. I would always beat it out of town before the werewolf got a whiff of me.

Cowardly? No, smart …from what I have heard of Vampire and werewolf confrontations.

One night: while running a saloon table in some small western town, I don't even believe it had a name it was so small, I got a whiff of something foul even before this hombre walked into the saloon. On the sound of the swinging batwing doors of the saloon, the odor got intense. (Batwing saloon doors: No pun intended. Most western saloons had swinging doors that were designed to allow a person to have a good look into a saloon before entering. The swinging doors were called Batwings due to their resemblance to large bat wings.)

I pretended to keep my attention on the game while splitting my attention to the foul smelling hombre that was approaching the bar.

With his back to me, the hombre announced for all to hear, especially me, "You stink, Gambler, In fact, you stink so bad, I could smell you while I was clear outside."

What do you say in a situation like this? I decided to ignore the hombre and faked full concentration on the game. It was clear that everyone at the table heard him, and they were becoming uneasy. It was the player on my right's move, and he'd suddenly become indecisive— possibly he was too interested in my next move, and I don't mean in the game.

The hombre turned slowly, and staring right at me, he continued, "Hey, fancy gambler, I said you stink like something dead!"

All the gamblers quickly withdrew from the gambling table except me. I just calmly placed my cards on the table, made a point of placing both my hands on the table, and stared back at him. That's when I observed something strange, despite his stink. He seemed to be calling me out, but he wasn't wearing a gun.

"I was about finished for the night, I'll leave …," I placated.

"To hell you say!" He suddenly lunged at me like a bobcat, his fingers changed to razor sharp claws of death, and his mouth became filled with fangs! All this happened so fast that a normal human most likely would not have seen it coming, let alone have time to draw his gun and empty six rounds of silver bullets into this creature from hell. Thanks to my supernatural Vampiric speed, I did! First, I pushed myself from the interference of the table and brought up my left-handed gun, the one specially loaded for just such an occurrence. I observed the first shot hit the werewolf through the forehead. As bullet and brains splattered the bar front, the other five shots ripped into his chest, and some forced their way out of the werewolf's back, splashing blood over the brain matter sticking to the bar front. One round got past him and over the bar to smash some liquor bottles, adding to the confused scene.

The werewolf hit the table with such force that all four legs broke into kindling. The table, cards, money and werewolf all crashed to the floor. From the blood pooling out from under the corpse, I didn't believe anyone would be playing with those cards again or having use for the blood-soaked money!

As the werewolf died before crushing the table to the floor, it transformed back to its human form before anyone, but me, even noticed any change in the appearance of the attacker.

When the sheriff arrived and asked for the facts, everyone proclaimed that the crazy hombre called me out and then charged at me. It was only then that it occurred to anyone that the dead dude apparently had no pistol or knife.

Personally, I was just glad I had already learned of the dangers of werewolves and had one gun properly loaded for the occasion!

Some decades later, after a bad night at the tables, I went to a Vampire Bar I had previously smelled out, for you can truly find a Vampire Bar from the intense smell of feeding, for a cheap meal on arriving in town …

I couldn't help but stare at the unusual tattoos this pale Vampire had all over his face and naked arms. Catching me staring, the pale stranger walked up to me and opened a conversation with, "I noticed you staring at my scars."

"Sorry, I didn't mean to stare ..." I stammered, feeling guilty as charged.

"No problem ..."

I couldn't help inquiring, "Scars?"

"Yes, scars I received from a hell beast called a werewolf." He continued, "A Vampire-hunting werewolf blew into town looking to destroy Vampires. Nobody even knew he was in town, no one even smelled him ... You know, you can always smell a werewolf, no matter what form they're in. But no one could smell this werewolf."

"Any idea why no one could smell this werewolf? I was told that Vampires can always smell a werewolf."

Shaking his head, he replied, "Some believe he had some magic something-or-other on him; some surmised he was too heavily perfumed to be smelled coming. No one really knows." The word was getting out that this hell beast was killing every Vampire in town, so a lot of Vampires split. I was in my room packing some things when this hell beast came crashing through my bedroom window. He was on me faster than I could respond ... his razor sharp claws ripped into me like an army of daggers. I was sure I was going to be his next victim, until I successfully withdrew a gun I had specially loaded with silver bullets."

"That was smart of you," I interjected.

"Aye, only the creature caught me removing the weapon from my pants pocket and grabbed at it. I thought I was a goner for sure and out of desperation, I started pulling the trigger. I just knew the gun wasn't pointed at the beast, but I had to do something, so I just kept pulling the trigger over and over again. The air between us was getting foul with gun smoke when the beast suddenly roared in pain and threw me across the room. I hit hard and blacked out, either from the pain of the attack or from hitting the wall, I don't know ..." He took a breather from his story telling.

"So, if you survived the attack, why didn't you regenerate and lose the scars?" I asked, perplexed.

"In telling this story over the years, some believe that the lack of a body must be an indication that I only winged the beast; hurting him, but not fatally."

He continued, "As to the scars, some believe the beast to have been a skin-walker … an Indian shape-shifter who uses magic. That could explain why no one could sense the beast and explain my failure to totally regenerate."

This story and others have convinced me that I don't want to mess with a werewolf.

Now, on arriving within a new town and getting the slightest whiff of a werewolf, *I'm gone!* I strongly suggest you, as a Vampire, do the same!

Vampire vs. Vampire

Do Vampires have to worry about Vampires hunting them?

Normally, no. *But ...*

I was at a Vampire Club one night when the word was getting around of a Vampire who was stalking Vampires and staking them.

It seems some Vamp got turned by her Vampire lover, and she wasn't happy. This Vamp had killed her Vampire lover in revenge for being turned without her consent. But she wasn't stopping there; no, she was out to kill all Vampires, especially male Vampires.

How was the problem solved? A Vamp who had been successful in getting away from the Vigilante Vampire turned the tables on her by tracking the Vigilante Vamp back to her resting place. She then called a Vampire Hunter she knew of and dropped the dime on the Vigilante Vampire.

This has to be the only time a Vampire called a Vampire Hunter to solve a Vampire problem!

CHAPTER 9
ANATOMY OF A VAMPIRE

To my knowledge, there has never been any scientific medical paper on the examination of an Undead Vampire. The rest of this chapter, particularly pertaining to the autopsy of the Undead, is hypothetical. Most likely the reason that no autopsy has been performed is the result of the use of fluorescent and ultraviolet (UV) surgical lighting.

The first time a dead Undead Vampire is removed from the protection of a body bag, the remains will explode like flash paper. Surgical theaters use lighting systems that include ultraviolet (UV) lighting. The purpose of the UV rays is to assist in the sterilization of the surgical theater. UV rays are also found in sunlight. By now you know what sunlight does to the Undead Vampire.

The science world tends to think of Vampires generally as fictional or mythical characters. How many examiners ingrained in science are going to admit that a patient exploded into nonexistence before their eyes. It's much easier on one's reputation and career to explain a missing corpse as a misplaced one, paperwork and all.

However *if* an autopsy *could* be done this is how it might turn out…

Humanoid Appearance
Legend has it that the first Vampire was the first wife of the first man on Earth. Some tales have it that she had a really superior attitude toward her having been created *before* Adam. Some tales have it that she had a real inferiority complex as she was created *after* Adam. Whichever the case, she was a real bitch.

God, giving up on changing her poor mind-set, threw her out of the Garden of Eden and replaced her with Eve. Later, for revenge Lilith—the first human wife—started feeding on the blood of Adam's children, and the first Vampire was born.

Whatever the case, looking like your prey does make hunting for a crimson dinner a lot easier.

Ectodermic System

At first sight, a dead human corpse will have the same blood drained appearance as a dead vampire (remains of living or undead) The blood within a human corpse will drain to the lowest part of the body, in this case, to the backside of the prone cold dead body. When surgically starting the autopsy, the first curiosity a medical examiner will discover is the abnormal toughness in cutting into the body. While the skin of a Living Vampire is a bit tougher than that of a blood bag, the ectoderm system is visually similar. The skin of an Undead Vampire is a great deal tougher as it has long been a dead system and simply hardened to a tough leathery shell of a skin.

Muscular System

Once past the ectodermic layer, cutting into the body will not get any easier. The tendons and muscles of a Vampire (living or undead) are much tighter than that of a blood bag. This is what gives a Vampire superior strength.

Cardiovascular System

Cracking through the ribs, the medical examiner will come to the heart. This is not the typical heart of a blood bag. At first sight, the heart of a Living Vampire will not look noticeably different; if the medical examiner is examining the heart of an Undead Vampire, the difference may be shocking. The heart of an Undead Vampire is smaller and darker than that of a typical blood bag's heart. Some romantics say the heart is smaller and darker because the heart is where the soul is housed, and an Undead Vampire has no soul. Try telling that to a dark-skinned Undead Vampire, such as an African or African-American Vampire! He may smash his fingers through your ribs, grab your heart and rip it out of you.

Then as you bleed your last, he will tear your heart open in front of you just to see if *you* have a soul. Then just to see if your shocked expression can get any more revolting, he will let you watch through dying eyes as he enjoys greedily consuming your heart for a lovely snack.

Truth is that an Undead Vampire's circular system is so sluggish compared to a Living Vampire or a blood bag's that the heart over time shrinks in size and becomes darker in color. The color difference comes from the fact that an Undead Vampire's blood is darker. This also is convenient in that it makes killing an Undead Vampire with a stake to the heart a little more difficult, since it is a smaller target.

Vampire blood does not regenerate itself through the lungs like that of a blood bag. It not only does not regenerate, but it burns off within the circulatory system and constantly needs to be replaced with fresh blood, hence the constant need and craving for fresh blood. If the medical examiner is examining an Undead Vampire, he will also notice the decrease in secondary or smaller blood veins; these veins have decayed from lack of use.

Respiratory System

If the cadaver is a Living Vampire, the lungs may not appear noticeably different, as a Living Vampire's respiratory system has still been in use. If the cadaver is an Undead Vampire, the changes in the respiratory system will be very noticeable. Undead Vampires don't breathe. They only need to breathe when communicating; such a Vampire needs to inhale air so they can exhale air out past their voice box to be heard while talking to others. Their lungs will look smaller, almost dried.

Digestive System

If the examiner is cutting into a Living Vampire, the digestive system will appear fairly normal. This is because a Living Vampire's digestive system is still functioning to some degree. Remember: A Living Vampire still needs to regenerate his blood from an external source, just not to the same degree as an Undead Vampire. This may be because a Living Vampire still has a working digestive system, and an Undead Vampire does not.

The digestive system of an Undead Vampire, like the Undead Vampire heart, will be seen as smaller, most likely from lack of use. The digestive system is dead. An Undead Vampire gets all it needs from the crimson fluid of life he takes from his dining. He can eat like a blood bag, but only to pose as one. Food consumed by an Undead Vampire goes straight through the stomach, into the intestines and out the anus without providing any nutriment to the body.

The medical examiner will find the small and large intestines of an Undead Vampire very strange; they are dead. There is a lack of any healthy bacteria that all Living Vampires and blood bags need to have to process nutritional food into molecules that the body can use. For Undead Vampires, the intestinal tubing has become hard and looks more like a vacuum cleaner tube than any living intestinal tubing.

If the medical examiner has not yet been stupefied by his Vampire cadaver, wait until he gets to the teeth, more to the point the maxilla, upper teeth and the canine teeth. If our examiner should start fingering the canine teeth—watch out! No matter how long a Vampire has been truly dead, if the examiner gets his fingers anywhere near the canines they will extract, possible knifing right into the examiner's finger, much like a dead shark may bite down on a arm after death—it's a reflex.

After our examiner has gotten over the fright of being attacked by his cadaver, further examination of the offending razor-sharp canine teeth will reveal that they are basically hollow with strong muscular veins that lead to the nostrils. When the Vampire was feeding, blood was forced up into the hollowed canine teeth by a series of muscles along the canine veins that push the blood into the back of the nasal cavity, down the throat and into the stomach to be absorbed into the feeder's system, to replenish the body with fresh living blood. Of course, while the canine teeth are absorbing the crimson fluid of life additional blood is gushing down the throat and into the stomach in a more traditional way of feeding. Nothing like a nice hot crimson meal to replenish the respiratory system and all its cravings—if only temporarily.

By the way, Vampire teeth are so strong that they never get cavities; the only reason a Vampire would visit a dentist is possibly to make a meal of said dentist. I have heard a tale of a newly turned Vampire that had an upcoming visit scheduled with his dentist. He totally relished pinning the man to his dental chair and with the words, "This won't hurt much!" He consumed the life fluids right out of his dentist. Afterward, he had the dentist's bitchy secretary for dessert. He told me, "I did consider leaving a bill for my services, but I figured that would be just a little too cheeky."

Reproductive System

While much has been said earlier about the reproductive system of the male and female Vampire, to a medical examiner the reproductive system of a Vampire cadaver would look unremarkable. If the examiner is experienced enough, he might notice that the reproductive system of this male or female has been dead a lot longer than the rest of the cadaver.

Hair and Nails

Even blood bags continue growing hair and nails for a time after death. As to how much hair an Undead Vampire continues to grow depends on the individual Vampire, much like some older blood bags continue growing hair while other older blood bags may lose hair noticeably. This might not be noticed by a medical examiner, but nails of an Undead Vampire may be another story.

While I have never met an Asian Vampire, nor have my travels taken me into any Asian countries, I have heard that Asian Vampires do not trim their nails, deliberately letting both hand and feet nails grow over the years. This raises a question: How do Asian Vampires get their shoes and socks on over extremely long nails? Possible answer: Some Asian Vampires are not Vampires as Europeans consider them, but spirits, like ghosts, that don't walk but glide a little off the floor. As I have said, none of this has been personally verified by me.

CHAPTER TEN
VAMPIRES AROUND THE WORLD

AFRICA

Is it all that surprising that as big a continent as Africa is, that there are so many different types of Vampires?

In West Africa, you can find the *Obayifo*, the Ashanti name for Vampires. These creatures attack people, especially children, for their blood. Neighboring tribes call them *Dahomeans* and *Asiman*.

The *Asasabonsamare* Vampires hang out on tree limbs and capture their prey with their long hooked legs.

Many African tribes have folklore of creatures that are Vampire-like by night and witches by day, sometimes secret witches.

Ewe people of Aclze have a Vampire who takes the form of a firefly. This creature seems to specialize in feeding on children.

The Betsileo tribe of Madagascar has the *Ramango*, reported to be Living Vampires who attack travelers for their blood.

NORTH AMERICA

Canada

Canada has stories of bloodthirsty Big Foots and Wendigos. These creatures seem more like Werewolves than Vampires.

Early French trappers tell tales of Vampiric loup-garou. A Loup-garou is a werewolf, so does this mean it is a Vampiric werewolf?

UNITED STATES OF AMERICA

The United States of America is a diverse nation made up of many cultures from around the world, so the USA Vampire is also diverse. The United States of American Vampire tends to be a basic European Vampire. Before United States of America was stolen from Native Americans, and turned into what it is today, there was a culture made up of various Indian tribes. (You do realize that even the term "Indian" is imported. The natives became "Indians" when the explorer Christopher Columbus landed near America and thought he was in India, so he started calling the natives "Indians.") Being big on skin-walkers, shape-shifters and ghosts, North American Indians weren't much into Vampires. Thus said I found this …

Jumlin

The father of all Native American Vampires, *Jumlin* was a demon that was called up by a medicine man to help in making his wife fertile when the Great Spirit would not.

The Jumlin fooled the medicine man, and the demonic spirit permanently possessed the medicine man and made the medicine man's wife pregnant. The Jumlin kept himself undead by attacking others for their blood. This Vampire not only had children from the medicine man's wife, but raped other women and had children from them.

The children grew up to be just like their dad, demonic Vampires who continued their immortal existence by attacking others for their blood.

With time, the Jumlin and his children moved from tribe to tribe, pillaging, raping and killing for blood. They would leave some of the raped women alive to raise more Jumlin children. It's believed that children of Jumlin exist even today.

For more on Jumlin and his children read, *The Lone Werewolf*, Melange Books, By Tim Forder.

U'tl't

The Cherokee have the legend of *U'tl't*, a female Vampire who stole and ate the livers of her victims without their knowledge. The victim would die a couple of days later. Eventually, when she was trapping in a pit, her reign of terror ended with an arrow shot into her hand, where her heart was located.

New England

I found tales of a colony of Vampires who came from Europe around the time of the Pilgrims to escape Vampire Hunter persecution. Historically, I could not verify any of this. The fact that I could not verify information of a Vampire colony is not surprising. They traveled a great distance to get away from Vampire Hunters; they would not have chanced attracting the wrong kind of attention from other colonies by attacking them for their blood.

I could see how a colony of Living Vampires could live happily catching live game to be exploited for their blood.

Rhode Island

In the late 18th century, and into the 19th century, the state of Rhode Island became known as "the Transylvania of America" due to an outbreak of tuberculosis, then known as "consumption." This airborne illness is very contagious, and takes time before symptoms are visible. When a family member died from it, later, additional family members would come down with it. This area was originally colonized by Slavic settlers, so it is not hard to see how his led to a belief that the newly-dead were rising up as Vampires and attacking their families. The belief in Vampirism was fortified when the newly dead were exhumed and appeared bloated with blood. Such bodies were then burned to ashes.

On the subject of the bloating of the dead, the appearance of bloating is a natural phenomenon from the buildup of decay gas within a body that is decomposing. It's not uncommon for dead bodies while being prepared for burial to fart or belch. You only have to worry if the dead body apologizes afterward.

Louisiana

In Louisiana, the French tell tales of Vampiric *loup-garou*. As a Loup-garou is a werewolf, this must be some form of a Vampiric werewolf.

Need I mention Anne Rice? Her Vampire tales have made New Orleans a Vampire mecca.

CENTRAL AMERICA

Haiti

A Loogarroo is a Vampire found on Haiti and other islands of the West Indies. This Vampire name is a distortion of the French Loup-garou.

Loogeroos are people who have made a pact with the devil. In return for immortality, they would share their nightly blood take with the devil.

Each night, the Loogaroo sheds its skin and travels the night in the form of a fiery ball of light. In this form, they can enter any dwelling not properly protected, and go on a blood feast with the occupants. This could be thwarted by placing sand or rice, mixed with nails, in the doorway. The Vampire would be forced to count the grains of sand or rice while trying to pick it up. The nails would cause the Vampire to drop his hold on the grains, and the Vampire would have to start all over again. Eventually, the sun rises and torches the creature of the night.

SOUTH AMERICA

Mexico

The *Camazotz* is an Aztec Vampire described as a "man-bat" with a very sharp nose, big ears, large teeth and claws. It's reported that it even has the ability to allow the head to fly separate from its body, by its large ears. Some believe these sightings of bodiless Camazotz to be sightings of a large bat indigenous to this region. It's thought that the belief in Camazotz spread out to neighboring Aztec tribes from a religious cult of the Zapotec Indians around 100 B.C. The cult worshiped an anthropomorphic monster with the head of a bat, an animal associated with night, death, and sacrifice.

Brazil

Lobishomen, a Brazilian Vampire, is described as a small, stumpy, hunch-backed, monkey-like being. It has a yellow face, bloodless lips, black teeth, a bushy beard, and plush-covered feet. It attacks females and causes them to become nymphomaniacs. Lobishomen are vulnerable when drunk on blood, making them easier to catch. It could then be crucified on a tree.

The *Pishtaco* is a Vampire that Brazil shares with Peru. This Vampire can take the form of a bat or a white man. Because of the Vampire taking on the form a white man, Spanish missionaries had difficulty in getting Indians to trust any white man. This Vampire is so thirsty he will attack someone for their blood and body fat.

Chili

The *Piuchen* is a shape-shifting serpentine Vampire who is highly feared in Chili. When flying, it makes a fearsome whistling noise that sparks fear in anyone who hears it.

Surinam

The *Asema* are Surinam Vampires who pose as old men or women by day, but at night shed their skin and fly about as balls of blue light. In their luminous stage, they can easily enter any dwelling to drain the blood of the occupants. This can be prevented by placing garlic around doors and windows. It's also suggested that you consume some garlic before bed, just in case one gets past your defenses; doing so will make your blood unpalatable to the Vampire, preventing the victim from dying from blood loss. One way to keep the Vampire from entering is to spread seeds or rice and iron nails mix at your doorstep. The Vampire will be lured into picking up the mix, piece by piece, in the pursuit of counting the mix. The nails will cause the Vampire to constantly drop his pieces, and the Vampire will be compelled to start over, again and again … until the sun rises, destroying the creature.

Another way to kill this creature of the night is to find its skin and apply salt to it, so that the skin shrinks to the point that the Vampire can't fit into it. Once the sun rises, the Vampire is destroyed by the morning's light.

AUSTRALIA

The *Yara-ma-yha-who* is a creature from Australia. This creature resembles a little red man with a very big head and large mouth with no teeth. On the ends of its hands and feet are suckers. It lives in fig trees and does not hunt for food. It waits until an unsuspecting traveler rests under the tree, then it catches the victim and drains their blood using the suckers on its hands and feet, making them weak. It later comes back and consumes the person, drinks some water, and then takes a nap. Later, the Yara-ma-yha-who awakens and regurgitates the victim. This then leaves the victim "shorter" than before. The victim's skin also turns slightly more "red" than before.

Sith, W. Ramsey. Myths and Legends of the Australian Aboriginals. Farrar & Rinehart; New York. p. 342

BULGARIA

A *Vorkolak* is the creation of a Vampire who was the victim of a wild animal attack. This Vampire will rise from the dead to haunt the area where it was attacked by blood feasting on anyone who enters its area. To put the Vorkolak to rest, one must find the Vorkolak's remains and have a priest pray over them, then place a cross over the area. While most Vorkolaks remain in the area where they were attacked and killed, some will leave their area to feed on their family and loved ones if the family lives close to the area where they were attacked and turned.

To Gagauz people, Vampires are *Obur*, renowned for their gluttonous blood drinking. Interestingly, they have the ability to move objects like a poltergeist, and they are capable of producing noises like firecrackers. People would try to rid their town of Obur by offering it rich food or excrement.

CARRIBEAN

Jamaica

The *Tobago* or *ol' Higue* is a Vampire who resembles the Loogaroo of Haiti. It leaves its skin at night, and makes its way as a blue ball of light in search of blood. Like its Loogaroo cousin, to get rid of the Vampire, find its empty skin and apply salt to it so that the skin shrinks too small for the Vampire to fit into, and come the sunrise, the beast is destroyed by fire.

Trinidad

The *Sukuyan* from Trinidad is a Vampire who resembles the *Loogaroo* of Haiti. It leaves its skin at night, and travels as a blue ball of light in search of blood. Like its Loogaroo cousin, to get rid of the Vampire, find its empty skin and apply salt to it so that the skin shrinks too small for the Vampire to return into, then just wait for the coming of the sunrise to roast the beast by fire.

CHINA

Figure 7 Hanzi for Vampire requires three symbols: First symbol: "Suck"; Second symbol: "Blood"; Third symbol: "monster, ogre, or demon"—Translation from Ellen Forder.

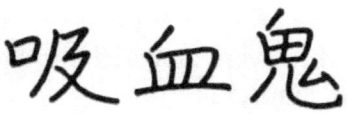

Jiang Shi are creatures of the night who suck the souls out of people while they sleep. These creatures are greenish skinned with long white hair. It's believed that they get their greenish skin tone from mold or fungus of the dead. Later tales of Jiang Shi portray them as "blood suckers;" The later tales of "bloodsucking" is believed most likely to be external contamination from Vampire tales from other counties.

K'uei is said to be a very vicious blood sucker, a part of a person's soul that has failed to pass on for various reasons, such as …

One who committed suicide

One who lived a very depressed life

One who lived a very deviant life

One who lived a very dishonest life

One who was not given a proper burial

One whose corpse was exposed to sunlight or moonlight

The latter two can create a *chiang-shih*, which is a blood sucker that has white fur all over and glowing red eyes.

DENMARK

The Mara is a beautiful woman by day and bloodsucking Vampire by night who attacks men. She especially likes to attack men who have declared their love for her in her beautiful form. Such creatures can be killed by a silver-bladed knife.

ENGLAND

During the 12th century, belief in Undead Vampires flourished in many parts of England. We know of this from the writings of three chroniclers who lived at the time: William of Newburgh (1136—c. a. 1200), William of Malmesbury (d. ca. 143), and Walter Map (d. ca. 1208). The belief at the time was that a corpse which left its grave at night to trouble the living was possessed and animated by a demon. This was usually the corpse of a person who had lived a sinful life.

One of the most interesting of these accounts is one of several reported by William of Newburgh. The main character in this case was that of a knight who had served the lord of Ainswick Castle in Yorkshire. The knight had led a lewd, wicked life. He died as the result of falling from the roof of his home, while spying on his own wife engaged in adultery. After his burial, he was seen again, prowling through the streets and around the houses in his village. His flesh was rotting and a plague resulted from the fetid air emitted from his decaying body.

The villagers finally destroyed this creature by exhuming the corpse and cremating it. They found the corpse to be ruddy and swollen. They attributed this condition to the corpse being bloated with the blood that it had drunk from its victims. The people then dragged the corpse to a place outside their village and cremated it. After that, both the appearances of the Vampire and the plague ended. In this account, William of Newburgh applies the Latin name *sanguisuga*, which literary means "blood sucker," to the Reverend.

FRANCE

Ancient France has no tales of Vampires, but they do have tales of people who would eat through their burial shroud and come forth in the form of a wolf, howling and consuming humans.

The fact that the French have tales of bloodsucking monsters, but don't have a Vampire name for them carried over to America, where they have Vampire-like creatures, which they call *Loup-garou* (French for Werewolf).

GREECE

Callicanzaros is a specific type of Vampire who attacks people between Christmas Day and New Year's Day. All are bloodsuckers, while some are reported to be cannibalistic. It's said that these creatures only attack at night, and after New Year's Day, they return to Hades to await the coming of the next Christmas Day.

To become a Callicantzaros you must have been born on or between the two holidays.

Lamias: according to Greek mythology, she was the first Vampire—an accidental creation of Zeus and his wife Hera.

Zeus had an affair with Lamia and begot many children. Hera, in a fit of jealousy, destroyed all of Lamia's children in front of her. Lamia, crazed with grief, started attacking any child she could find by draining them of their blood. For fun, she started destroying men's marriages and then she'd suck the men dry. If she failed to ruin a marriage, she would still suck the man's blood.

Lamia then started creating more of her own kind, called Lamias. It's believed that they are even now out destroying marriages and men!

The island of Crete has their own Vampires called the *Katthakanas*. It is a basic Vampire, except to destroy this Vampire, you have to decapitate it and purify the head in boiling vinegar.

GERMANY
Figure 8 Two Alps tormenting a sleeping beauty; Wikipedia, Public Domain as copyright has expired

Nachzehrer are German Vampires who were persons who died of sudden causes like suicide or accidental death. It was common practice to hammer a nail down the head of someone being prepared for burial, just to be sure the dead would stay in the grave. Nail down the head meant to literally pound a large nail into the mouth and through to the coffin or grave dirt to ensure the corpse stays buried.

The *Blautsauger* (German for "bloodsucker)" is the southern German (Bavarian) equivalent of the

Nachzehrer. If a Blautsauger was suspected of being in the area, the locals would spread garlic around the outside of doors and windows and keep Hawthorne plants inside their residence. If a person owned a black dog, extra eyes would be painted on the dog to help scare away the Vampire. Such Vampires could be killed by staking or/and decapitation.

The *Alp* is an interesting Vampire/incubus-like creature. The Alp is reported to rest by the side of its sleeping victim and give them nightmares. Alps are male so they mostly attack women in their sleep. While Alps like to terrorize their victims during sleep, they do need to feed and they are reported to feed mostly off the breasts of their victims for blood, but will also feed off the beasts of victims for their breast milk! It's reported that an Alp can be found out because they eventually get emboldened enough to sit on the person they are attacking.

Alps take on the form of normal person by day, so the way to find an Alp is to mark it during one of its attacks and look for that mark on the people around you by day. Alps don't roam far.

Protections against an Alp include laying a broomstick under a pillow, iron horseshoes hung from the bedpost, placing shoes against the bed or placing a mirror on the chest. Steel and crosses are also used. Keeping a bedside light on may help.

To rid yourself of an Alp, have a person stand guard, covertly, so they can jump out and mark the Alp.

Alps are reported to be nearly impossible to kill and scaring one off by marking it may cause the Alp to make reappearance in the future in a nastier mood.

INDIA

In India, there are ancient writings about Hindu Vampires called *Vetalas*, a ghoulish creature that inhabits corpses of the dead. They are sometimes reported to be found hanging upside down from tree branches in a graveyard. These bloodsuckers were evildoers or insane when alive.

Churel are believed to be women who died in childbirth or passed away while menstruating, hence their need for blood! Churel appear as old women with large sagging breasts or as young voluminous ladies. Their first victim is usually their husband or love interest; after sucking him dry, they then move on to any man available.

Tim Forder

A *Chedipe* is a succubus/Vampire. If she sees a man who interests her, she will walk into the house by night, usually naked. She will enthrall the whole household and have her sexual pleasure with the man. Afterward, she will feed her need for blood from the man's toe. If she likes the man, she will not feed to the point of death; she'll just get more blood from the rest of the entranced family! She'll then leave with the plans to return the next night. In most cases, the man will not even know what has happened; he will just awaken a bit weaker each morning until he finally dies a slow death from blood loss or sickness as a result of the feedings.

Rakshasa is a Hindu bloodsucking demon. Most likely, this bloodsucker resulted from someone who was evil before they died. A Rakshasa may be female or male.

These creatures may be shapeshifters or may appear to be shapeshifters due to their ability to be an illusionist.

Apparently, Rakshasa are not bothered by holy symbols, as they commonly haunt or terrorize priests and worshipers at holy shrines.

IRAN/IRAQ

Iran/Iraq has a Vampire called the *Ekimmu* that goes back to ancient Babylonian history. This creature of the night goes underground by day and comes out at night to feed off the living.

"Ekimmu" means "that which is snatched away." Basically, Ekimmu are creations of violent deaths, such as …

Improper burial
Lack of offerings during burial
Died of unrequited love
Died a violent death

You know you have an Ekimmu problem if your luck has gone south, and you hear the Ekimmu howling at night!

Another creature from the Mesopotamian area is the Vampire-like creatures called the *Uruku* or *Utukku*. The Uruku is actually referred to as a "vampyre which attacks man" in a cuneiform inscription. There is very little known about the Uruku.

IRELAND

Dearg-Dul, Dearg-Dur, Dearg-Dililat and *Dearg-Diulai:* A dreaded creature of Ireland whose name means "bloodsucker." An ancient Vampire who dates back to Celtic times, it is still feared even today. The only way to curb its appetite is to pile stones on the grave suspected to be housing such a beast.

-Internet: World Vampire Myths

ISRAEL

Aluga is the Hebrew word for "horse-leach" from Proverbs 30:15 and Latin for "bloodsucker." This Vampire is sometimes considered to be a very intelligent bloodsucking demon; always described as very tall (over six feet), with white complexion, and very formidable fangs.

Estrie is a female Vampire who prefers feeding off children, but will feed on whomever is handy if no children can be found. An Estria is normally seen in the form of a beautiful woman, considered her best form for enticing children to come close to her for feeding. She has the ability to sprout large wings for flight.

Motetz dam is Hebrew for "bloodsucker". This is an ancient demonic Vampire who is so feared that little can be found about it.

-Internet: World Vampire Myths

ITALY

A *Strigio* is a Vampire of Roman mythology. The Vampire name was originally called *Stix*. Strigio in human form has red hair and blue eyes. They have the ability to shape-shift into many animals at will.

One interesting reason a corpse may become a strigio is if the corpse feels unfulfilled because death came before marriage. For this reason, there used to be a tradition of having a marriage service with another corpse for the recently departed.

To keep a Vampire from rising, it was common practice to place rings of garlic within and on the coffin.

The traditional ways of dispatching a Vampire work fine with strigio.

NORWAY

*Gjengangar*is a ghostly Vampire, human in appearance, except for the long claw-like nails and the fangs! These Vampires go way back to Viking lore.

Gjengangar arise from the grave if they committed suicide or had unfinished business, usually revenge!

Gronnskjegg (Grons-jeg) translates to "ghoul" because it is a Vampire created from a human that feeds like a ghoul when alive by committing cannibalism. It's reported that this Vampire can change its form to look like someone else for the purpose of enticing its next blood feast.

JAPAN

Figure 9 Kanji for Vampire, requires is three symbols: First symbol: "Suck"; Second symbol: "Blood"; Third symbol: "monster, ogre, or demon"—Translation from Ellen Forder. Kanji, the Japanese name for Chinese writing system, is one of three writing systems used in Japan.

Japanese folklore includes an aquatic Vampire called a *Kappa*. Looking like a human tortoise, the Kappa have been reported as being seen coming out of a lake, pond, river or any other form of water, to pull cows and horses into the water where the animal then is drained of its blood. Some tales have Kappa enticing men and women to the water's edge, then pulling them into the water to drain them of their blood. Some tales have Kappa raping women before relieving them of their blood!

And then there is this ...

The "Vampire Cat of Nabeshima" is the story of Prince Nabeshima and his beautiful concubine Otoyo. One night, a large Vampire cat broke into Otoyo's room and killed her in the traditional manner. It disposed of her body and assumed her form. As Otoyo, the cat began to sap the life out of the prince each night while guards strangely fell asleep. Finally, one young guard was able to stay awake and saw the Vampire in the form of the young girl. As the guard stood by, the girl was unable to approach the prince. The prince then slowly recovered. Finally, it was decided that the girl was a malevolent spirit who had targeted the prince. The young man, with several guards, went to the girl's apartment. The Vampire escaped, however, and removed itself to the hill country. From there, reports of its work were soon received. The prince organized a great hunt, and the Vampire was finally killed. The story has been made into a play, *The Vampire Cat* (1918), and a movie, *Hiroku Kaibyoden* (1969).

MALAYSIA

Langsuir are vicious female Vampires who are women who died in childbirth. Forty nights after burial, a langsuir will rise with a thirst for blood and a vengeful craving to get that blood from men. This femme fatale can change her appearance to better entice men to their death!

Their natural appearance is reported to be hideous, scary, vengeful and furious. The *langsuir* is further characterized as having red eyes, sharp claws, long hair, a green or white robe (most of the time), and a rotten face with long fangs. It's reported that they have the ability to fly.

Supposedly, if you can catch one and cut their hair and claws, a langsuir will become human again. To prevent a langsuir from rising from the grave, just place beads in the woman's mouth as part of the burial preparation.

Figure 10 Penanggalan; with permission of artist Sammi Bold

Penanggalan literally means "head with dancing intestines" as this Vampire is a flying female head, spine, stomach and intestines. While Penanggalan prefer the blood of newborns, anyone with blood can be a victim. This Vampire can come out by day disguised in a complete body.

THE PHILIPPINES

A *Manananggal* Vampire differs from its Penanggalan cousin in that this Vampire's total upper half detaches and sprouts huge bat wings for flying around. This Vampire also goes by the name tik-tik, for the sounds its wings make in flight.

POLAND

Vjesci, Vampire of northern Poland, will awaken at midnight after their burial and feed off their family until the family no longer exists. The Vjesci will then move on to feeding off neighbors. Survivors can end the blood feast in the traditional ways.

If you believe a person will rise again, you might prevent it by placing a crucifix in the mouth of the person being prepared for burial, then place a net over that personage. If through movement the crucifix should be removed, the Vampire will not be able to leave its coffin until it has untied every knot in the net, which is a *very, very* slow process.

The *Upier* Vampire is considered to be an extremely vicious Polish Vampire. It will first attack children and then continue on to kill the parents. Strangely, this Vampire rises during the day and sleeps at night, and in doing so has a fairly human appearance. It needs to collect lots of blood, because it feels the need to sleep in a pool of blood. This may explain its vicious nature.

PORTUGAL

Bruxa is the Portugal cousin to Bruja found in Spain and means "witch." A Bruxa is a woman by day and a bloodsucking Vampire by night. This beast has the ability to transform into various animals and has a thing for infants. While it prefers infants, anyone with blood could be a victim.

ROMANIA

Nosferatu is a species of Vampire, said to be the illegitimate child of parents who were illegitimate. Soon after its burial, the Nosferatu embarks on a long career of destruction. It delights in tormenting and engaging in wild orgies with the living. The male can father children. The Vampire hates newly married couples due to its own illegitimacy, and wreaks its revenge on such couples by making the groom impotent and the bride barren.

Drakul is a Vampire possessed by a demon. Of course, this is Dracula country. The people of this region have many Vampire stories to tell. There is hardly a family around that doesn't have a Vampire story or two to tell.

Many people in this region live off the tourism trade of Transylvanian Vampires and Count Dracula fame.

RUSSIA

Upyr Vampire is considered to be extremely vicious. It will first attack children and then continue on to kill the parents. As with the *Upier*, the Upyr rises during the day and sleeps at night, and in doing so has a fairly human appearance. It feels the need to sleep in a pool of blood. This may explain its vicious nature.

SCOTLAND

Baobhansith (pronounced *baa'-van shee*) is a female seducer of men. The Scottish Highlanders call her the "the White Woman," This seductress tends to be found in forested areas where she finds a man to tempt with dance, and then, she had her fun: making a blood feast on the man drawing his blood through her fingernails.

SPAIN

Bruja is Spanish for "witch". A Bruja is a woman by day and a bloodsucking Vampire by night. This beast has the ability to transform into various animals and has a thing for infants. While infants are preferred, anyone with blood can be a victim.

THAILAND

PhiiKrasue "head with dancing intestines" is a flying Vampire female head, spine, stomach and intestines! While PhiiKrasue prefers the blood of a newborn, anyone with blood can be a victim.

During the day this Vampire can come out into the sunlight in its complete bodily form.

TURKEY

Vourdalak is a re-animated, un-decayed, bloodsucking dead person, most commonly returning to prey on its loved ones. A Vourdalak is normally a woman out to attack men.

Wurdulak is a highly-feared Vampire that first returns from the dead to attack its family and then moves on from there.

WALES

Craitnag Folley (meaning "Blood Bat") is a basic European Vampire.

Soodar Folley (meaning "Blood Sucker") is another basic European Vampire.

WALLACHIA

A *Muroni* is reported to be a Vampire that has the ability to change itself into a variety of different animal forms. While in one of these incarnations, the Muroni can kill easily, and leave misleading signs of an animal attack. It totally covers signs of a Vampire attack, with the exception of the total blood loss—if anyone cares to note!

VIETNAM

Incus (In-cus) is a vampiric creature that drains humans of their blood through an antenna that grows out of its nose.

YUGOSLAVIA

Vukodlak originally referred to a werewolf (a rough English translation is "wolf's hair"), but somehow over time it has came to refer to a fairly typical Dracula-type Vampire. A local variation of the legend states that instead of (or sometimes in addition to) drinking their blood, the Vukodlak will engage in sex with young widows or with women who were girlfriends or wives when the Vampire was a normal blood bag (human being).

CHAPTER TEN
A LITTLE VAMPIRE HUMOR

Have you heard about the Vampires who twinkle in the daylight? Seems someone put the bite on Tinkerbell.

A Vampire walked into a bar and ordered "Type O." The bartender ordered him to leave, seems the establishment didn't serve his type!

Did you hear that Corday, the Vampire's girlfriend, left him? Seems he was a real *pain in the neck*!

A Vampire walks into the local blood bank and left soon after very disappointed … seems they would not let him make a withdrawal!

How many Vampires does it take to replace a light bulb? NONE; what Vampire needs the light on?

Hear about the gay Vampire Hunter? He really loves his work!

Have you heard the joke about the priest, the Jew, and the Vampire? Neither have I!

A Vampire once died from shock from just reading his mail. He discovered he had won the sweep*stakes*!

What's the last thing a Vampire will order off a restaurant menu? *Steak* and potato!

To all those I have known over the years and will know in the future ... *Fangs for the memories*!

Bloody good humor, what!

GLOSSARY

Billy the Kid. Born: William Bonney (A.K.A. Billy the Kid) was born in 1859 and died in 1881 at the age of 21. Bonnie lived in New Mexico and Arizona areas in the 1870s, He not only had criminal ties to these states but had criminal ties to Texas as well. I fudged history a little in have the fun of including him in this story for the enjoyment of you readers.

Blood Bag: Shortened Vampire terminology for Walking Blood Bags, also known as humans. Basically this is how Vampires see humans … *as food*!

Bone cutter or Saw bones: War time surgeon. The name "bone cutter" came about because amputation was the most common surgery of the Civil War.

Bouncing Betty: S-mines created in the late 1930s by Germany. This defensive weapon was heavily used during WWII as an anti-personal mine. American soldiers were the ones who gave the S-mine the name Bouncing Betty, because the mine was designed to bounce about 2 to 3 feet up, then explode for maximum effect. The Bouncing Betty was so successful, other countries started designing their own versions.

Complete meal: Vampire terminology for blood feasting to the point of the death of the walking blood bag.

Dracul: 1) Romanian for "Devil" or "Dragon/Serpent"; 2) a historic Romanian prince given territories that buffered the known civilized world from the barbaric world of the Turks; 3) Slavic term for a Vampire possessed by a demon.

Dracula: 1) Romanian for "Son of the Devil" or "Son of a Dragon or Serpent;" 2) Historic prince who inherited his father's kingdom and responsibilities; 3) famous fictitious Vampire character created by Bram

Stoker. See Dracul.

Duster: Long coat worn "on the trail" to keep the trail dust off the rest of your clothes. Horseback riding can be very dusty traveling depending on the trail or the circumstances, such as moving herds. Dusters can be a handy way for modern day Vampire Hunters to carry their tools of death hidden within pockets under the long coat!

Fallen doves: Old West term for what the good book would call a prostitute. Also known back then as soiled doves.

Enthrallment: A form of advanced controlling hypnotism used to enslave a person, persons, or animals to do a Vampire's bidding. Enthrallment of animals may be where the misconception that all Vampires can transform into animals came from.

Lucifer: 1) Old West terminology for a wooden match stick. Cardboard or pressed paper match sticks hadn't come to be yet; 2) Name for the Devil, Satan, etc.

Mound of Venus: an Old English phrase, still used in the Old West, for that part of a female anatomy between the legs. I have heard it referred to as "the place man comes forth at birth, and spends the rest of his life trying to get back into!"

Moving Pictures: Old name for a form of entertainment that become "movies." The first movies were just that, moving pictures seen by flashing a number of still pictures making the numerous still pictures look like moving pictures.

Soiled doves: Old West term for what the good book would call a prostitute. Also known back then as fallen doves

Turn or turning: The process of changing a walking blood bag into a Vampire. This is accomplished through the sharing of blood between a Vampire and a walking blood bag.

Walking Blood Bag: Vampire terminology for humans. It's how many Vampires view humans … AS WALKING FOOD CONTAINERS!

Figure 11 Vampire Dolls Property of author.

Pleasant Nightmares!

Bibliography:

Neurology 1998;51:856-859.
Sith, W. Ramsey. Myths and Legends of the Australian Aboriginals.
Farrar & Rinehart; New York. p. 342
Internet: World Vampire Myths

List of Sources:

Property of the author:
Figure 1 Vampire Beauty.
Figure 11 Vampire Dolls Property of author;

Wikipedia, Public Domain as copyright has expired
Figure 2 Lilith
Figure 3 Vlad Tepes, better known as DRACULA.
Figure 4 Wood Carving of Vlad the Impaler at work a.k.a. Dracula,
Figure 5 ERZSEBET (ELIZABETH) BATHORY
Figure 6 Bram Stoker
Figure 8 Two Alps Tormenting a sleeping beauty
Figure 7 Kenji for Vampire
Figure 9 Kenji for Vampire

Commishioned work
Figure 10 Penanggalan; with permission of artist Sammi Bold.

About the Author

Timothy (Tim) Forder was born and raised in Maryland, USA. It's my mother's theory that I get my love of horror and fantasy from being born just a couple of blocks from the gravesite of Edgar Allen Poe in Baltimore!

I'm a very happy family man with a family consisting of a beautiful wife, a creative teenage daughter, (live-in) sister-in-law, Seeing Eye Dog and daughter's rabbit.

For some years now, I have been losing what little eyesight I have left to RP (Retinitis Pigmentosa). If you need someone to talk to about coping with vision loss or Seeing Eye Dogs feel free to e-mail me at Facebook.

I have been a huge fan of the horror and fantasy genre, specially the older material, since my pre-teen years. I was introduced to the genre by the family sitter. Sue and I had an agreement: If I didn't beat up on my sister I could watch Creature Feature with her, which was past my bedtime and after my sister went to bed. I will never forget Sue Greenspan's words of wisdom: "Remember, what you see in the movies is only make believe and can't hurt you." Years later, I was the man when my buddies and I would go see Hammer Horror movies at the local theatre, and I would sit in my seat laughing at my friends as they tried to take cover from the horror on the screen! Sue Greenspan, if you are reading this thank you for many fun filled hours with my monsters!

Started my college studies in Wildlife Biology. I wrote a thesis on Dracula that was picked as the year's best work. I was given the honor of reading the thesis to the class, and by sundown, the paper was both famous and infamous around campus! As a result, on campus my nickname of "Tex" (because of my flare for western hats) became "The Vampire".

A bookworm from my early years, I still consume books like food, only being blind, most of my books are compliments of The Congressional Talking Book program (books on special cassettes or the newer digital books for the visually handicapped).

Other works by the author at Melange

The Lone Werewolf

www.ingramcontent.com/pod-product-compliance
Lightning Source LLC
Chambersburg PA
CBHW031840170626
46807CB00004B/1543